SPA SHADOWS

Jennifer J. Morgan

Books by Jennifer J. Morgan

Libby Madsen Cozy Mysteries

Shadows in the Forest
Spa Shadows
Shadowed Treasures (summer 2022)
Shadow Retreats (fall/winter 2022)

The Christmas Fairy - a holiday novella

SPA SHADOWS

Libby Madsen Cozy Mysteries, Book 2

Jennifer J. Morgan

Secret Staircase Books

Spa Shadows
Published by Secret Staircase Books, an imprint of
Columbine Publishing Group, LLC
PO Box 416, Angel Fire, NM 87710

Book layout and design by Secret Staircase Books
First trade paperback edition: July, 2022

First e-book edition: July, 2022

* * *

Publisher's Cataloging-in-Publication Data

Morgan, Jennifer J.
Spa Shadows / by Jennifer J. Morgan.
p. cm.
ISBN 978-1649140944 (paperback)
ISBN 978-1649140951 (e-book)

1. Libby Madsen (Fictitious character). 2. Arizona—Fiction. 3.
Amateur sleuths—Fiction. 4. Women sleuths—Fiction. I. Title

Libby Madsen Cozy Mystery Series : Book 2.
Morgan, Jennifer J., Libby Madsen cozy mysteries.

BISAC : FICTION / Mystery & Detective.
813/.54

For my husband. Our adventures together mean everything to me. Thank you for helping me become the best version of myself. I love you beyond measure.

PROLOGUE

Akron, OH - 1986

They were just children. Milo and Chester spent the long hot summer of 1986 locked away in a juvenile detention center. It wouldn't take long before these two were inseparable.

Milo was the oldest at thirteen and this was his second stint in juvie. His first offense was theft, and no fault of his own—the two older kids he was with were arrested for armed robbery; he was an accessory, even though he hadn't stolen a thing. Once released back into society, continuing to run with the wrong crowd, it was evident that this would be his way of life. This time around, he was incarcerated for auto theft, armed robbery, and assault. One thing he knew for sure, his time spent initially taught him all about the correctional institution. He learned how to fly just under the radar, to not be noticed by the older kids. On occasion, however, he would have to flex his muscle to show the others who was boss. He wasn't a bully, but the best way to keep the bullies off his back would be to stand up to them. Milo wasn't a large kid by any means, but he could fight. This time in the system, he would be in for a while—might as well establish his territory early on.

Then Chester was admitted to Milo's same unit. The scrappy, ginger-headed, ten-year-old walked in with his shoulders slumped, staring at the ground. Right away Milo knew this kid would have it rough. His size for one—scrawniest little thing. But, also, it was how he held himself. He was timid, shy, and wouldn't look anyone in the eye. Poor kid. He had no idea what he'd gotten himself into. The two shared a bunk—Milo on top and Chester on the bottom. The first night all Milo could hear were sniffles. Yep, the kid was doomed in a place like this.

A couple nights later, right after lights out, Chester finally said his first words.

"Whatcha in fer?" the barely audible voice whispered.

"I stole a car. Mighta beat someone, too," Milo whispered back.

"Hey, shut up!" someone in the next bunk over yelled.

Those were the only words spoken that night, but it would open a door of friendship for months to come.

One day Chester came back to the bunks with his face all torn up. Someone definitely used him as a punching bag.

Milo asked, "Who did that?"

"Ah, no big deal. No one," he said with his head down, no eye contact. He felt his face and already he knew his eye would be swollen shut within the hour.

"You gotta fight back, ya know," Milo said, demonstrating with a few air punches and his face scrunched up like a tough prizefighter. "I bet it was that wuss, Tony the phony, huh? I pounded his ass. You tell me and I'll go remind him whose friend you are."

Chester chuckled and glanced up at Milo. That was the most eye contact the two had during his first week in the joint, but it was the beginning of the rapport between them.

Every day was the same routine. They woke, ate the cafeteria slop, cleaned up, sat in 'school', went outside a couple times a day, and then back to the bunks. They were kept busy to keep them out of trouble, but that didn't matter, the boys in this place were always looking to make trouble. Milo and Chester stuck together and, for the most part, the older kids stopped picking on the younger one.

Until one day when Chester went to shower alone.

"Hey, Howdy Doody! Where's your boyfriend?" Tony jeered.

Chester startled, but didn't look at the kid, he just kept moving toward the shower.

"Hey! I'm talking to you, punk. Don't ignore me!" Tony pushed Chester into the stall door. "Where's your boyfriend?"

"Milo's still asleep," Chester's small voice quivered.

Three more from Tony's gang appeared in the doorway. One closed the door, then stood guard. The others, along with Tony, surrounded Chester and backed him into the corner of the shower.

"Let's teach him good." The larger, overweight kid pushed him.

Chester fell to the ground, hitting his head against the tiled wall. Fists began slamming him in the face before everything went black. Time stopped.

Just outside the bathroom, there was a loud crash. Then the door sailed open and Milo charged into the room. Lifting the closest boy to him, Milo thrust him across the room and then proceeded to do the same with the others, until he came to Tony.

"Ah, came to rescue your little boyfriend, did ya?" Tony spat.

"Get away from him now!" Milo screamed. He was trying to gain the attention of guards he'd hoped were in the hallway by now.

Tony puffed his chest, posturing. Milo reached out and grabbed his collar, pulling him in closer and quickly punching Tony in the face, throwing him against the wall opposite from Chester. Tony gave up; Milo rushed to Chester. He was unconscious and splayed out on his stomach with his clothes ripped off. Blood was everywhere. Milo rolled him over and saw that most of the crimson was coming from his nose and a head wound. Gently, he enveloped his friend into his arms.

With his voice cracking, he whispered into the small boy's ear, "Why didn't you wait for me? Why?" He lifted the limp body and ran for help.

After a day in the infirmary, Chester was back in the bunkroom.

"Hey, kiddo. You okay?" Milo asked as he saw the bruised and swollen redhead crawl back into his bed.

"I'm fine," he said quietly.

Milo crawled down out of his bunk, kneeled onto the floor in front of Chester, and looked the kid in the eyes.

"Those punks will never touch you again, I assure you of that."

"Did you get in trouble?" Chester meekly asked.

"Well, yes. But, not as bad as the others. Ya know, was told not to fight anymore, got a little more time, but they understood I was trying to save you. You were in bad shape, brother."

Chester's eyes found the floor again. He was ashamed. "Thank you, Milo. I'll never forget what you've done for me here."

"Hey, no problem kiddo. You'll always be a little bro to me." He slapped the side of Chester's arm and hiked back up to his bed.

Neither ever spoke of the incident again, and no one bothered Chester again before he was released from detention six months later. Milo had several more years to serve.

After Chester was on the outside, they kept in contact, writing letters to one another. Chester was tossed around between foster homes endlessly and struggled. His letters to Milo were getting more desperate sounding as the years passed.

By 1991, Milo was released from the institution and his juvenile records were sealed. He realized unless he took action to change things, he would spend the rest of his life in prison. He decided to join the Army. Although never truly doing well with authority, he managed to serve his time and was released honorably. In the years following, he thrived … found himself a decent job, a wife, and they went on to have three children. Life couldn't have been better.

Once Milo left the military in 1996, he searched for

Chester only to discover that he was in prison—statutory rape. It'd been ten years since Milo last saw his little friend when he decided to pay him a visit. Chester wasn't so "little" anymore. All grown up, he was a strapping six foot tall and two-hundred pounds. On that visit, Milo learned the full story.

At eighteen years old, Chester thought he found the love of his life. He was happy and they were in love. Come to learn she was only fifteen years old. Her father was livid when he learned of his daughter's boyfriend's checkered history, so he pressed charges and now Chester was serving time—three years and a lifetime with 'rape' on his record.

Even though Milo was no longer physically worried about his little buddy, he still offered him some sound advice.

"Bro, you don't have long in here. When you get out, you need to get your life together. I served in the military—it saved my life. That may or may not be your calling, but seriously, think about what you'll do different when you get out. And, remember, I'm always here for you." Milo couldn't hug Chester in the guarded room, but the look they exchanged conveyed the same message.

One year later, Chester was released from prison, but remained on the registered sex offender list—something he would have to learn to live with. Since his visit from Milo the previous year, he had joined a men's Christian ministry in prison and accepted the Lord Jesus Christ as his savior. This proved instrumental as he assimilated back into civilian life. Serving on a mission, he moved to Mesa, AZ and met his future wife at church. Life was finally looking up.

* * *

Twenty Years Since Juvie Days
2006

Chester's wife turned up the volume on their TV. "Ches! Did you hear about this?"

"What!?" he yelled from the other room. He walked into the living room and stared at her.

"Look …" She pointed at the TV, where the perky reporter was handing the story over to another reporter in Ohio.

Neighbors were horrified yesterday in the normally quiet Akron suburb when a house abruptly went up in flames. It has since been learned that firefighters found a grisly scene—three children and a woman's remains were discovered and they're calling this a homicide. Question is, where is Milo Robinson? The father, and husband, is nowhere to be found. Police say he is a person of interest. He is a known outdoor enthusiast and survivalist. If you've seen this man, please call your local police.

Chester watched in horror. His best friend—what on earth happened?

CHAPTER ONE

Summer 2020

My new roommate, Isobel Crenshaw—who has informed me she prefers her nickname, Bella—was adjusting well to her new normal. Several months had passed since the ordeal with leaving her abusive childhood behind. She was diligently working at weekly psychotherapy and seemed to be doing well.

"Ready for your first day?" I asked.

"I really appreciate this, Libby. You and Alexis are so kind giving me a job." Isobel's smile lit up the room. She was excited to get started.

"Hey, you interviewed for it—we didn't just 'give' it to you," I reminded, giving her a quick hug. "Can you let Shadow out one last time? I'll get us some travel mugs for our coffee."

Shadow came bounding into the room as soon as she heard her name and 'out'. I grabbed a few things from the fridge. Several pieces of lunchmeat, a couple string cheese packets, and an apple. From the pantry, I grabbed the large container of mixed nuts and then threw everything into my tote bag. *That will have to do for sustenance today—it's going to be a busy one!* I poured two travel mugs with my favorite coffee blend and tightened the lids.

"Wow, Shadow has so much energy this morning!" Isobel commented, laughing as she nearly got bowled over coming through the back sliding glass door.

"Yeah, I'm not loving the fact we weren't able to go on our run this morning. I overslept, and I have a completely full schedule today."

I grabbed two treats for Shadow, locked the back door, and called my canine friend over to her kennel. "Good girl! I'll come let you out in a little while. Be right back," I said in my best soothing voice as I threw the two cookies to the rear of the crate. She didn't look thrilled, but she did jump right in after those treats.

Isobel and I loaded up in my silver Toyota 4-Runner and set out for work. My adulthood dream had always been to own a spa business—and now I've done it! Well, my business partner, Alexis, and I have opened *our* dream business—the Dharma Inspired Day Spa. Opened for two years now, but recently the emergence of the COVID-19 virus had us shut down for nearly six weeks. We made ends meet by offering home visits for well-known and established clients. Thankfully, the governor has now cancelled that mandate; we're back to business.

"Did you hear that story in the news last night about a serial rapist in the east valley?" Isobel asked, breaking into my thoughts as we drove down the road.

"No. What's going on?"

"Well, they said there are now four women who have reported being attacked … in their bedrooms during early morning hours."

"Holy crap. Really? Here?"

"Mesa, Chandler, and I think one occurred in Tempe, too. Anyway, just be careful. I know you love jogging really early in the morning to beat the heat. Although, I think these are cases of breaking into homes—just be careful anyway."

We pulled into the parking lot at the spa within five minutes of leaving home. Yes, we could even walk here from home, but not in July. Not in Arizona, it's simply too hot.

Isobel surprised me when her left arm suddenly crossed in front of my face. "What's that?" She pointed to the front of the building. It looked like Alexis beat us here; she was standing out front staring at the glass windows. We parked, grabbed our stuff, and walked up to the building. On the glass was painted what could have been gang graffiti, except for the clearly written 'LESBOS' in bright fluorescent pink across the front door. Didn't look like any gang graffiti I'd seen in other parts of town.

"I've already called the police." Alexis didn't even look at us, she just kept staring at the vandalism as she spoke in a monotone voice.

"Wha…What? How…?" I was stunned at what I saw.

"Hopefully the cameras we installed caught whoever did this," she added. Then she turned to us, "Oh, I'm sorry. Good morning, ladies!" She gave us each a hug.

"Let's wait for the police inside. Have you touched the front door?" I asked Alexis.

"No. Just got here and I only pulled out my phone to take photos and make the call." She reached into her purse and grabbed a small eyeglass wiping cloth. "Here, let's carefully use this to open the door. Don't touch anything."

Once we got inside, the three of us inspected every room. We checked all the doors, windows and everything was secure—no one had tried to break in, thankfully.

The police arrived to take our statements. They checked the footage from our cameras. Luckily, our cameras are located inside the building and pointed outward so the vandals couldn't get to them. Unfortunately, the lighting was not great in the front of our building. We could see a shadowy figure, dressed all in black, and apparently wearing a face mask. The person was tall, not short and there was not even one bit of footage that showed the person's face. The stature led us to believe it could be a man. But, that was it. Not extremely helpful.

After the police left, I turned to Alexis and Isobel, "Let's get busy cleaning that mess up, customers will be arriving within the hour."

"Oh, let me do it, Libby," Isobel piped up immediately. "Really, it's my first day. I'm great at cleaning. Besides, you two need to get set up for your clients."

"I think I'm going to like this arrangement," Alexis said with a huge smile.

"Thank you, Isobel. Let me show you where the cleaning supplies are. After my first client, I should have more time to get you acquainted at the front desk."

* * *

By the time my first session was completed and I walked my client, Michelle, back to the front desk, Isobel had the windows perfectly shiny and new. I checked Michelle out while taking the opportunity to instruct Isobel on our software and training her how to schedule the next visit. She was a natural.

"You sure look comfortable behind the desk," I commented. "And hey, great job getting those windows cleaned. They look fantastic!"

"Thanks! I love it here already—I mean, what's not to love?" Bella's eyes shined, showing her smile clearly even behind her face mask. "Seriously, I'm so grateful."

"Follow me, I'll show you what needs to be done before the next appointment. If someone walks in the door, we'll hear the ding in the back," I said, as we walked through the frosted glass doors into the Serenity room.

Alexis' client was relaxing with her eyes closed on the plush sofa near the fountain when we walked through. We stayed quiet until we made our way through the next set of doors and into the therapy room I had just used. I proceeded to give Bella the rundown of what she needed to do after each massage: strip the linens and scour all surfaces with disinfectant (including doorknobs, light switches, etc.).

"Refill this essential oil diffuser," I demonstrated. "And take these linens into the laundry room, rotating the loads throughout the day."

"With the virus protocol, is there anything more that I need to consider when cleaning?" she asked.

"Great question. Mainly, we need to disinfect all touch surfaces after each client leaves. Right now, we're scheduling appointments with a lot of padding between so there should never be more than one client in the Serenity room at a time. We might have a client leaving and one arriving as you just saw, but in general, there won't be more than a couple clients at a time in the building."

"There's so much space; I would think that's sufficient."

"Yeah, it's been working well. Just remember whenever you aren't checking someone in or out, there's always something to do. Also, in the Serenity room, make sure there's always plenty of hot water in the heated carafes and a nice assortment of herbal teas."

I left her to start the laundry and I stepped into the office to double check my schedule. My next client enjoys Ashiatsu, which is massage that I perform with my bare feet. No, I don't walk on people's backs, but I do stand on the table, using my feet to obtain a deeper tissue massage. The clients love this modality, and using multiple methods has definitely helped me to slow down the effect of repetitive motion strain on my hands. I checked my watch—one more ninety-minute appointment and then I could run home to let Shadow outside.

By lunchtime, we were the only three left in the building so we gathered in the Serenity room on the floor pillows where each of us stretched out and rested.

"Why on earth would someone spray paint the front of our business?" Alexis sighed and took another sip of her herbal tea.

"I thought this was the good part of Mesa," Bella observed. "I didn't think there was crime on this side of town."

"I think there's crime everywhere, but generally, I haven't had any issues since moving to the east valley." I set my mug down on the coffee table. "Oh, shoot, I've gotta go let Shadow out."

"Is she allowed to be here at the spa?" Bella asked.

"Oh yes, I usually do have her here when I don't have so many back-to-back sessions."

"I'll watch her if you want to bring her back with you," Bella suggested.

"Ok, she'd *love* that! I'm outta here ... see you in a few."

* * *

Shadow was beyond ready to be rescued. She came bounding out and we headed straight for the back door. She ran immediately to the far end of the wall, where she began her usual reconnaissance of our backyard. The entire perimeter was thoroughly inspected, especially the back gate that led to the front yard. Once she had done her business and was satisfied that all was secure, we played ball for a few minutes. She's so fast that she's generally right under the ball by the time it gets to the other end of the small backyard. So, recently, I've started to fake the throw. She gets all the way to the other end, then I toss it behind me so she has to run the length of the yard again. My girl loves this game—the smile on her face as she runs for the ball is priceless.

The other thing she absolutely loves is a car ride and an afternoon greeting customers at the spa. Bella and Shadow have bonded quite nicely since she moved in so this should work great when I'm in a session with a client—Bella will definitely have a shadow wherever she goes.

Alexis was at the front desk assisting Bella when we walked in the front doors.

"Shadow! Sweet girl!" Shadow found her way around the counter and relished all the love she got from my friends. Looking up at me and then over to Bella, Alexis said, "How about you guys come over for dinner tonight?

I have some salmon and lots of fresh produce for a big salad."

"Sounds perfect. What time?" I asked. Bella nodded her head in agreement as well.

"I think we're both out of here around six, right? Let's say seven then?" We all agreed and then went about the rest of our day.

We pulled up to the Johnson's house right at seven. They lived in a nice neighborhood southwest of where our spa was. Their light gray stucco house with pillars at the front door and beautiful desert landscape all around was customary for the area.

"Libby!" JJ gave me a huge hug after he opened the door. "Great to see you, ladies. Good evening, Bella." He moved out of the doorway and we walked through into the large great room and kitchen area where Alexis was already pouring the Sauvignon Blanc.

"Aunt Libby!!!" Joshua came running in from the other room and jumped into my arms. I loved and kissed on my godson and then set him back to the floor, where he ran off and jumped onto the sofa, grabbing his game console. Bella followed him and asked if she could play. He got really excited that an adult would have any interest in his game.

"So, what's been going on in your world, JJ?" I asked as I took a sip of wine.

"Oh, you know … just trying to keep law and order. All in a day's work." He laughed and followed me to the breakfast bar where we sat and helped Alexis chop vegetables.

"Honey, don't be so modest. Tell Libby the great news,"

Alexis coaxed him to share.

"Well, nothing is for certain. They have me working with the homicide detectives, looking to solve a fourteen-year-old murder that occurred in Akron, OH."

"Ohio? Why would a Mesa police officer be working on a murder in Ohio?" I asked.

"It's a cold case and they're considering me for a detective position. This particular case has come back to light because there have been several recent sightings of the suspect in Arizona. Why they picked me? I have no idea."

The look Alexis gave her husband said it all. "Oh, love, you truly don't know what we all value in you, do you? You are the hardest working, most ethical and upstanding officer in this community. I *know* I'm biased, but your fellow officers and superiors continually sing the same praise, too." She blew him a kiss across the countertop.

He blushed. "It would be really cool if I got promoted to detective, wouldn't it?"

"JJ, I think all of this is fantastic! And deservedly so." I reached over and gave a little side hug.

From the sofa, Joshua starting chanting, "Dad is great! Dad is great!" Bella was laughing and doing a little dance sitting in place.

Alexis came around the counter and stood in front of her husband who was still sitting on the high-top stool. She reached her hands on either side of his light brown crew-cut hair, gently massaging his temple area. "Well, I definitely think a promotion is a great thing. I'm proud of you whether or not you get it. However, I am a little concerned whether this type of case will take you away from home more often. And, I do worry about how they will take their toll on you. Mentally." She brought his head closer and gently kissed his forehead.

"Ahhh, you two are way too sweet. Gag!" I mimicked shoving my finger down my throat. Laughing, I topped off our wine, and then followed JJ outside as he took the salmon to the barbecue grill.

"How's Greg? Talked to him recently?" JJ asked about my new forest ranger friend. Ok, *boyfriend*. We are classifying ourselves as such these days. Although it has taken awhile, we have moved beyond the friend stage and are now in the early developments of a relationship.

"He's super busy right now with fire season. You know, there are now four different fires in the region? Terrifying, I tell you. And, maddening. I'm so tired of learning that unmanned campfires are the cause." The heat flushed my cheeks.

"Oh, wow. I heard of the one close to Show Low, but didn't realize there were others. That's gotta be tough. But, you know, there's nowhere he'd rather be than helping the community, right?"

I agreed. "Definitely. He's right where he's supposed to be."

"The salmon is ready. Let's go eat." JJ smiled and we headed back inside.

We gathered at their dining table and loaded our plates with fresh salad and a piece of salmon each. I was surprised to see the five-year-old enjoying it too. I don't know a whole lot about kids, but I can tell you that my sister's children would never touch fish.

"What type of marinade is this on the salmon?" Bella asked Alexis.

"I put together a hot-honey glaze. Let's see, I whisked

together honey, sriracha, whole mustard seed, and soy sauce."

"Delicious!" I managed to say as I enjoyed another bite.

"Libby told us you're starting school soon, what are you taking?" JJ asked Isobel.

"Yes! I'm very excited. I decided I want to get certified as an EMT and the East Valley Institute of Technology has a 16-week course there."

"And you were able to qualify for a grant, isn't that right?" I added.

"Yep, it was something my therapist told me about so I applied, got accepted, and now I start classes shortly."

"Libby and I did our massage therapy certification at that school, too," Alexis added. Then she looked to JJ, "I told you, Bella is helping us at the spa now, too, right?"

"Yeah, yeah, you did. How's that coming along, Bella?" JJ asked.

"First day was great!" she said, but then her face took a turn. "Except for the graffiti tagged on the building. What is that about anyway? I don't understand people who damage property by writing on it. It's never made sense to me."

"Oh, by the way … Officer McLaughlin was the one who filed that report. I was talking to him during break today and I guess they weren't able to tell much from the camera. That's disappointing, I thought we got those hung where they'd be most effective at the door." JJ set his glass down and helped himself to more salad before continuing. "Let's look at that tomorrow and I'll get some better lighting installed."

"I'm just praying it was a one-time incident—punk kids who will move on to a different area. I don't think we have any reason to believe we were specifically targeted, do you?" I asked Alexis.

"I hope not. Then again, what was 'Lesbos' about?" She turned to JJ. "That's what was written. Well, there were other symbols or markings, but that's the only part legible."

"That's odd. Maybe whoever did it knows two women own the spa and are making assumptions?" JJ's eyebrows arched upward in question.

"Who knows? Let's just pray it doesn't happen again."

"That reminds me, Lib, please be careful jogging in the morning." JJ looked at me pointedly. I set my glass down. "There have been several *incidents* lately. I'll give you more details after little man here goes night-night."

"Oh! Right. Bella was saying something about that earlier." Both Bella and I exchanged a look, remembering the newscast she had heard about a serial rapist in the east valley. "Yep, I do carry pepper spray and try to stay aware of my surroundings. I'll be careful."

Out of the blue, Joshua piped up smiling really big. "I go to school. I go to Miss Gartner's class. We color. We play. I no work." We all laughed at the seriousness in how he described his class. It was obvious that he had waited his turn from when we mentioned Bella going to school. So adorable, and he loved being part of adult conversation, so we asked all about his teacher and what they were learning in pre-school. I took a sip of my wine as I watched everyone interacting. I just love this family—Alexis and JJ are very engaging parents. They are incredible friends. If I could do it the way they are, I might even consider doing this parenting thing someday. As it is for now, I love my life exactly as it is.

CHAPTER TWO

A few days later, still no update from the police, but business was back to busy—almost pre-pandemic level.

"Hey Alexis," Bella said as she walked into the office later that evening, "I got the laundry done, folded, and linens are stored in the cabinet. Front register is shut down. I've disinfected everything. Unless you need anything else, I'm going to head out. First night of classes."

"Oh, wow, bet you're excited. No, I'm just about done here myself and will be headed out, too. Enjoy class and we'll see you tomorrow."

"Ok, goodnight," Bella yelled as she disappeared through the door.

Five minutes later, the door chime sounded. Alexis was

alone. She was typing entries in her bookkeeping software when there was another chime. Expecting to see Bella coming through the door again, she was shocked to see a large masked man.

Alexis immediately stood up. "We're closed." When it was obvious he wasn't going to stop, she started frantically searching for a possible weapon. "What do you want?"

He reached into his pocket and pulled out a gun as he rushed forward, lunged, and grabbed her arm. "Good. Then we have the place all to ourselves." The sneer in his voice sent chills through her body. His piercing green eyes were pure evil.

"What do you want? You can have the cash from the register … come, let's go get it." She calmly tried to distract him, even though her heartbeat skyrocketed and her palms became clammy.

"Shut up! You whore!" he screamed, and pushed her into one of the massage rooms, slamming her to the table.

"Wh…what? Why?" she cried, as she scrambled to sit up.

"You move in here and soil our neighborhood! This, this … sex business. You whores will pay!"

"We … it's … not a sex business. We're therap…"

"SHUT UP!" he screamed directly into her face. "You are the scourge of the earth. YOU are defiling our neighborhood and we want you to shut this business down."

"Ok. Ok. I understand." She'd do anything at this point to calm him. "Just let me go. I promise we …."

"CLAM IT! Only I do the talking around here, got it?" She nodded her head and lowered her eyes. He pointed the gun at her right temple "First, you are going to perform your *therapy* on me." He spat.

Alexis' pulse increased. She couldn't catch her breath and tears started flowing down her cheeks. Knowing better than to say anything else, she just sat there. The masked man started taking off his black long-sleeved shirt. She briefly looked up and saw that he had a large decorative cross tattooed over his left pectoral.

"Well? Don't you have to get some oil or something? Get moving! I want one of your best massages—Now!"

She slowly got up and carefully moved toward the cabinet and sink. Just as she was opening the cabinet to get the lotion, she swore she heard the front door chime. Alexis looked over at him to see—had he heard it?

He was glaring at her; his back was to the doorway. "What? What is taking so long, you slutty nig…" At the very moment he was shouting obscenities at her, Shadow appeared from nowhere. Growling with her teeth bared, the big dog jumped at him, knocking the intruder to the table. His gun fell to the floor. Panicking, he grabbed the gun and his shirt, and bolted out of the room. Shadow chased him right out of the building.

"Alexis!" I yelled out when I didn't find her in the office. Shadow's bark was urgent, unmistakable that something was very wrong.

Who was that? Someone just ran out the back door!

"Libby!! In here!" Alexis was breathless, struggling to scream. All the stress suddenly rendering her weak. "Libby!"

I found Alexis on the floor in the therapy room. She was crumpled up, hugging her knees, crouched into the far corner near the cabinetry. Shadow was sitting right next to her trying to lick her tears.

"Are you okay?" She nodded her head.

"Call 9-1-1. Make sure all the doors are locked, Libby."

I dialed as I ran to the back door. It was closed and required a key to unlock from the outside so we were safe there. With my heart racing, I ran to the front door and cautiously looked through the window outside. Even with the parking lot light, I couldn't see anyone. I locked the door and ran back to Alexis. Shadow hadn't budged; she was sticking by Alexis no matter what.

I gave the emergency operator our address and reported the armed robbery. The police were on the way.

"Oh, sweetie, what happened?" I crouched down on the floor next to my friend and wrapped my arms around her. Shadow bounced around, excitable now that we were all down at her level. "Did he harm you?"

The tears started pouring—she was sobbing. Eventually, she answered, "No. I'm okay. Terrified. He had a gun. He was screaming at me—calling me horrible, filthy names." Her sobs overtook her breathing and I just rubbed her back as she fought to catch her breath.

"Lexi, look at me," I said, gently trying to lift her chin with the tip of my finger. "It's going to be okay. Let's not touch anything, but make our way to the Serenity room where we'll be more comfortable. The police are on their way." She slowly came to standing. I took her quivering hand and led her to the sofas. I poured her a cup of chamomile tea and pulled a fluffy cashmere throw over her shoulders.

Keeping an eye on the front door, I opened it to the policemen when they arrived. As I was locking the door again, I heard JJ. He was running from the parking lot. "Libby!! What happened?" The expression on his face was pure terror. "Where's Alexis?"

"Come on in …" I led the policemen into the Serenity room. JJ immediately ran to his wife and took her into his arms. She began crying again. The female officer sat across from Lexi and waited to let her calm down before asking her questions.

I offered to take the other officer to the therapy room where I had found Alexis and I showed him the door where the perpetrator exited. He asked me several questions.

"I'm sorry, I really don't know much. I know my dog jumped at the man and then he ran out. I called you, and I haven't got much out of Alexis since. She's very shaken up. She did mention something about a gun and that he was calling her filthy names." I walked back to join the rest of the group, while the officer continued his investigation.

When I walked into the room, Lexi was opening up to the female officer and JJ was holding one hand and gently rubbing her back. Shadow was curled up at her feet.

Alexis turned to ask me, "Did you get a look at the intruder? Did he pass you as he ran out? I'm sorry, but I just couldn't remember how it all happened."

"Oh, sweetie, don't worry—this has been traumatizing; of course, you don't remember. Unfortunately, when I walked through those doors there," I pointed behind me to the doors that led from this room into the therapy, laundry, and office area, "he was already to the back door and I just saw that it was a fairly tall person. I don't think he had a shirt on. His back was pasty white. He was carrying stuff in his arms, but I have no idea what. I didn't see a gun."

"He held it to my head, right here," she said, pointing two fingers to her right temple. JJ squeezed her hand, then stood up agitated, and moved to join the other officer at the back of the building. My heart went out to both of my friends. Lexi was distraught and JJ looked as though he could kill someone.

After we wrapped up with the police, JJ and I gathered Alexis' belongings, shut off the lights, and we all walked out to the parking lot together. They left Alexis' car and she climbed into his Camry and locked the doors. He walked me the few spaces over to my car even though I told him I was okay. Forever the gentleman, that's my friend, JJ.

As I was loading Shadow in the back seat, JJ reached out for my arm. "Libby, I didn't want to upset Lex any further, but Officer Gonzales showed me something he found outside the back door." He swallowed hard. "Libs, there was rope … essentially, a *noose* laying just outside the door." My friend started to tear up. I hugged him.

"I don't even know what to say. This is shocking—I'm still stunned over finding Alexis like this." I took a deep breath. "I'm going to try and get a good night's sleep and then I'll come to your house in the morning, if that's okay?" He agreed.

* * *

Bella was home when I walked in. Shadow bounced over to her with gangly legs and spring-like steps. "Hey girl, where've you been … it's pretty late," she talked sweetly to Shadow, rubbing her behind the ears.

"We had a break-in at the spa, Bella … and Alexis was held at gunpoint," I blurted out. Then, I collapsed to the couch, broke down, and cried. How I'd even held it together this long, I really don't know, but in this moment, everything hit me—hard.

Bella kneeled down in front of me and Shadow was

immediately in my lap trying to kiss my face. "Wha …what? What do you mean? She was going to leave soon after I did." Her face contorted, worried. She stood up, hands on hips, and started pacing. "Uh, Libby … I, er, I'm afraid it may have been my fault."

I didn't understand. "How could it be your fault?"

"I don't remember locking the door. It was after hours when I left, but I don't remember using my key to lock the door when I hurried out to get to my class." She slumped into the chair across from me.

"Bella. It's not your fault that some nut job terrorized our friend. So, don't go down that path." I realized I was somewhat short with her, but I was exhausted. I didn't need any more drama this evening. "I know I just dropped a lot for you to absorb right now, and I'm sorry. I just need a hot bath and I need a good night's sleep. Please don't beat yourself up. We'll talk more in the morning, okay?"

She came over to hug me. "Of course. Get some sleep. I'll take Shadow out while you're in the bath. She probably needs to be fed too." Shadow was hesitant to leave my side, but the outdoors was calling her too so she eventually gave in and followed Bella.

My phone started to ring. It was Greg.

"Hi there," I said, trying to perk up so he didn't detect anything was wrong.

"What's wrong, Libby?" *Well, that didn't work. Guess I won't be changing my day job to actress.*

I couldn't help it. It was difficult to say the words out loud again, so I just started to sob. Eventually, I was able to coherently get the day's story told.

"My God, Libby. Is Alexis okay?" he asked.

"Physically, yes. She's okay—traumatized though.

I'm headed over there in the morning to be with her. We decided to close the spa tomorrow. She may be off a little longer than that, we'll see." It crossed my mind then that none of us were safe there. A whole new level of despair washed over me.

"Well, hey … on my next day off, I'll come to the city. Anything you guys need, I'm here for you. Please remember that." My wonderful forest ranger boyfriend— so comforting! Since the time we first met, several months ago, I have counted the blessings that he was brought into my life. I was doing a favor for one of my clients at the time, looking for her daughter up in a campground near where I usually spend hot summer days, when I met Greg Lawson. He helped me find Isobel and during that process, we became very close. I realized in the months since that we value the same important things in life: coffee, wine, good food, great friends, and we're both outdoor enthusiasts. "Libby, are you still with me?" he added.

"Oh, sorry. I drifted, I guess. Just marveling that I've only known you a few months, yet it feels like we've known each other forever. Thank you for being you." Tears came to my eyes again. "I would love to see you soon. I know you have your hands full there with the fires though, and really, I'm okay. Today was a difficult one—yes. But, tomorrow will look up, I'm sure."

"I'll be there as soon as they give me a day off. Promise." We talked for another half hour and I listened to his firefighting tales and the massive operation that was going on up north of the city. I really did miss seeing him in person.

CHAPTER THREE

It was five in the morning when the light started to filter through the blinds. As I lay there, all the horrible scenes from last night rushed back in my head. *Who would try to harm Alexis? And, most importantly, why?*

I got up to make coffee and let Shadow outside. No sense lying around wallowing in sadness. *I've got to do something.* I put on my yoga pants, a tank top, and my trainers and took Shadow on a run while the coffee brewed.

The sun was barely starting to peek out from behind the Superstition Mountains to the east. We lived in a master planned community at the northeast edge of Mesa that was backed up along state trust land where we were free to roam through the desert trails for miles. Today, we decided to stick to the city streets for our run. We headed west along

Thomas Rd. and made our way to another neighborhood about a mile away, then wound through the streets until we made our way to Higley Rd. before turning and heading back toward home.

Some people were already starting to leave for work, but mostly, the traffic was quiet. It was in the mid-eighties and only getting warmer as the sun started heating the asphalt. On the way home, we passed by the spa parking lot. Shadow abruptly stopped, which nearly sent me sailing over top of her. Thankfully, I managed to side-step around her and not fall.

"Shadow, what are you doing?" I realized she was just staring at the spa building, more than a hundred yards from where we stood. "We'll go there later. C'mon." I gently tugged the leash and motioned to keep going straight ahead on the sidewalk. She would not budge. Now, it's true, she's just a pup—about nine months old now, but she's also solid muscle. When she gets stubborn like this, there is no moving her easily. She continued with her nose pointed toward the building.

"Okay, we'll go that way." After all, there were multiple ways we could get home and apparently, she wanted to take the route that passed my workplace. So, we started running again. She took me directly to the back door and started sniffing intensely.

My pulse picked up, and it wasn't because of the running. I was uncomfortably aware that there were very few people out this time of morning and I felt like we were sitting ducks. What if the masked man returned? "C'mon, Shadow. We need to get home now."

Turning to leave, I caught a flash of something at the end of the building opposite from where we stood. Shadow was more than willing to sniff her way on down there as though she was the one who discovered a treasure. I bent down and picked up an ornate metal lighter. Turning it over in my hands, I saw that it had a 'W' engraved on one side and a beautiful cross on the other. Immediately realizing that this could be evidence, and regretting that I already handled it, I quickly used the bottom edge of my tank top to carefully wrap and tuck it just inside the waistband of my yoga pants. With no pockets, that's the only thing I could do. We took off for home.

Bella was enjoying coffee as we walked in the door. "You two are up early. Nice run?" she asked.

"Yeah, felt great to clear the head. Shadow found something out behind the spa building." I grabbed a paper towel and a plastic baggie from the pantry. Then, I gently removed the lighter from my yoga pants' waistband. With the paper towel, I put the lighter into the baggie and sealed it up. "I've got to get this to the police. Maybe the gunman last night dropped this in his hurry to get away?"

"Wouldn't the police have discovered it last night?" Bella asked.

"You'd think." I shuddered to think that someone came back after we were gone, but that was certainly a possibility, too. "Hey, we need to cancel all appointments for today, I'll get you the list from my laptop. Can you please call them with the news and reschedule? I'm heading over to Lexi's this morning and then we'll come up with a plan for reopening."

Bella looked disappointed. "Absolutely! And no worries, I have a little homework to do. And I have my therapy session later this afternoon. Otherwise, I'm here if you need me. Please give Lexi a hug from me. My heart breaks for her."

* * *

Alexis Johnson has been my friend for more than a decade and I've never seen her anything but happy, gracious, kind, and compassionate. From the moment I met her during our massage therapy schooling, she was always the one lifting everyone's spirit. She's always looked on the bright side of any situation and has always demonstrated absolute peace in her heart. Today was no different.

She greeted me at the door with a warm embrace. "My friend, you are the very person I need today," she said. I followed her inside and to her living room. She already had tea brewed and some fresh warm blueberry scones. We sat and enjoyed the treats silently for a bit.

"You look amazing this morning, Lex," I quietly commented between bites.

"Nothing that a nice long meditation session this morning couldn't heal." She smiled, that beautiful wide smile that lit up her smooth brown complexion, and made her eyes shine brightly.

"I don't know how you do it. I meditate and I just don't seem to get the same effect that you do."

"It's okay. It'll come to you when you need it most." Alexis turned more serious. "My faith, and meditation is a large part of that, has always healed and comforted me. *That's* how I do it."

"Where's Joshua—still asleep?" I asked.

"Ha! No, JJ took Joshua to the station with him this morning. He's just finalizing some paperwork and then they're headed to the Bounce House a little later to wear off that five-year-old energy and give mom a little break."

We sat and talked all morning. Eventually, she filled me

in on everything she had told the police. "I'll never forget his piercing green eyes. Ever." We discussed when we'd reopen and what we could do to improve security. At the end of it all, we both agreed that we couldn't run scared or let this change our lifelong dream. This was a deranged man who needed help and he would not deter us.

"If you're good being on your own today, Lex, then I think I'll head over to my mom's house. She called earlier and couldn't figure out something on her computer so I offered to help."

"Ah, good ol' Julia Madsen. How's she been anyway? I haven't heard anything about your mom in a while."

"Oh, well, prior to the pandemic, she *was* quite busy with her Leisure World retired set of friends and I hardly heard anything from her. They were constantly involved in *something*. Oh, remember, earlier this year, she went with a whole group of ladies on a European river cruise."

"That's right. I do remember that. She is a spunky energetic 70-something, isn't she?" Alexis giggled. "I hope I have half her energy when I get to her age."

"I know! Me too." I got up to rinse my plate and teacup in her kitchen sink. "Well, I don't think the pandemic has been doing mom any favors though. She doesn't like being holed up. She wants to travel and meet up with her friends for lunch." I moved back to the living room to pick up my purse.

"Hopefully, it won't be too much longer. They're talking about a vaccine before the end of the year," Lexi commented.

"Yes, I can't wait to have things get completely back to normal. Ok, my friend, I'm headed out. If you need *anything*, please call me."

"I'll be fine, Libby. Thank you for being here this morning—I really appreciate you." She got up and walked me toward the front door.

"Hey, I'll see you tomorrow!" I said as I left the house.

* * *

My mother lives about five miles away, which is very handy. For such a large city, my family has always remained within about a ten-mile radius. We've stuck close to one another since my dad died when I was sixteen. We're a close family, but as with any, we have our issues too. For one, Jordan—my older sister, is perfect. She is the perfect wife, mother, sister, and daughter. At least, according to our mom she is. My mom always seems to remind me of that—*Jordan is a master chef. Look how well-behaved my grandkids are—Jordan is a great mother. When are you going to get married, have kids?* Of course, Jordan isn't actually a chef and yes, she's a good mother, but she has her own set of issues, too. As anyone would. I love my sister. I don't love constantly being compared to her, though. We're so different.

"Libby!" Mom exclaimed as she opened the door and whisked me inside. "Come out of that heat and let's get some iced tea."

When mom suggests having something to drink or eat, there isn't any debate. You just pick from her offerings and don't even think of saying no; it's far easier to just accept and say thank you.

With our iced teas in hand, we proceeded to the living room where she started telling me all the neighborhood happenings. We sat on one of the two sofas she still had from the nineties when I was young. Covered in a brown, red, and orange floral pattern and displaying cushions that sagged from years of children and grandchildren abusing them, she wouldn't consider parting with this furniture. The room was complete with a long coffee table between the two sofas that faced one another, a piano in one corner, and two armless beige chairs that sat right in front of the huge picture window looking out onto the front yard. She lives on a corner lot and the house is positioned where you see the intersection and many houses up and down the street. I suppose it's perfect for her because she definitely spends a lot of time in this room, spying on neighbors.

"And, I tell you, they are up to no good," she was saying. "Those backpacks, they're young … what are they doing in this neighborhood?"

This was her latest kick. Apparently, she's been watching some young people riding their bikes up and down her street. Personally, I don't see the problem, but I just nodded and listened.

"Now, Doreen says she keeps seeing shady characters meet them at the corner. The one right up that way …" she pointed to my left, or west. "Margie says they are dealing drugs."

"Who's buying in this area?" I asked. "This is a 55+ community."

"Exactly. They are too young to be messing about in our neighborhood. I can't imagine who is buying around here, but I suppose some of these young ones are selling to each other. Cops aren't driving by often, that's for sure. Maybe they feel safer doing it here?"

"I'd think that'd make them more noticeable. Like you said, they're not living here since they are under 55." I set my tea down on the doily. "Now, what computer problems are you having this week?"

"Oh, there are messages that keep popping up. I don't know what to do about them. I've started calling this thing the 'confuser' … it confuses me *all the time*."

I laughed out loud at the expression on her face when she talked about her *confuser*. It's not as though my mother was really old. Aren't the seventies the new fifties? She's vibrant and fun, travels with a set of women from Leisure World, plays bingo regularly, and hosts cocktail hour at her home frequently. Since March, she has been mostly isolated at home. Jordan and I are really the ones who visit regularly and even then, Jordan has been keeping her four kids away from mom until the vaccine is available. Don't get me wrong, though, she talks endlessly on the phone with her friends. And she will stand in her yard and talk with neighbors from a distance so it's not like she has had absolutely no interaction.

"Ok, let me take a look." We stood and made our way to her second bedroom, which she uses as part hobby room and part office.

As we walked into the room, I marveled at all the fabric everywhere. There were bolts of every color and pattern you could imagine. She had her sewing machine front and center, along with shelves and baskets loaded with sewing supplies. Then in one corner, there was a very small desk with her computer. Clearly, the hobbies were taking over and the occasional accounting jobs she took on were becoming less and less. Good for her.

I booted up the computer and immediately saw what must be bothering her. I simply explained to her that she had some software updates that needed to be run. I clicked a few buttons and made it start updating while she showed me her latest quilting project. Once the update was done, I showed her what to do if she saw the messages come up again. I know better than to think she'll remember, but that's okay, she was listening intently.

"Would you like more iced tea?" she asked me.

"I have to get going, Mom. Unless you need help with anything else?"

"No, no. I know you're busy." *Oh, here comes the guilt trip.* "Jordan brought me a load of her great cooking. I have several homemade pot pies—chicken, beef, and pork—all in the freezer to eat when I need. She's such an amazing cook." *Why, why is this always a subject that comes up?*

"That's great, Mom. You're right, she takes good care of you," I said, giving her a hug and started to venture toward the front door.

"When are you getting married and settling down?" *Yep, here we go. Can't have one visit without talking about my lost soul.* "You need stability."

"Ok, Mom … I hear you. I've gotta go. I'll be back in a couple days. You take care, love you!" I said, and walked out the front door.

I have a successful business, amazing travels, overall, a wonderful life, and I don't need to be married to fill some void. I've never understood why that is so important to her. And, comparing me to Jordan … she seems to constantly forget that my sister is divorced now. Is that really what my mother wants for me, too? Sheesh.

I still couldn't believe there would be drug dealing going on in this senior community, but I decided to take a look for myself. I pulled out of my mother's driveway and drove down her street where she had earlier pointed to one of the 'drug' houses. When I got to the intersection, I turned right and drove slowly. There were two young guys riding their bikes on the other side of the road headed toward me. They both had backpacks on. When I got to the next block north, I looked down that street and saw two more bikes with riders that had backpacks on and riding away from me as I passed by. I suppose it is strange that people this young—I'm guessing late teens, early twenties—were riding bikes through this community. And, it's late July so school isn't in session. Otherwise, perhaps they could be taking a shortcut through the neighborhood on their way to school. I don't know. They certainly don't appear to be harming anything by just riding down the road. Mom needs something more to fill her days, I decided.

On the way home, I stopped by the police substation to turn in the newly acquired potential evidence I'd been carrying in my purse. When I walked in the front door, I immediately recognized the female officer who was interviewing Alexis last night. Now I realized her name tag said Officer Talin. The night she spoke with us was such a blur, I didn't even remember her introducing herself.

"Good to see you again, how may I help you, Libby?" she asked.

"Good morning. Um, my dog and I were jogging this morning," before I could continue, she interrupted.

"Please be careful out there jogging, there is a serial rapist that we haven't caught yet. Most of the cases have happened in real early morning hours."

"Yes, I'm aware. My dog is pretty good at alerting me to danger. Anyway, she—Shadow—led me to the back door of our spa building. Down near the corner of the building, I saw something flash in the sunlight and we discovered this." I pulled out the baggie from my purse and set it on the desk. "Unfortunately, I picked it up and handled it before I realized it could potentially be evidence from our intruder."

Officer Talin picked up the bag and turned the object over examining it. "Hmm, 'W'? It's a nice lighter, isn't it?" she said looking up at me.

"Have you had any leads on the case yet?" I asked.

"Unfortunately, the rapist case has taken most of our resources. No, I'm afraid to say, is the answer."

"Do you suppose the person who attacked Lexi was the rapist?" The thought just occurred to me.

"We're looking into that. I can't give too much detail, but there are aspects of the case that lead us to believe they are two different men. We just really don't know at this stage." She picked up a sheet of paper and asked me to fill it out. "We'll submit this into evidence. If you can just fill in some details here about when and where you found this lighter, that will greatly help us. Also, to rule your prints out, I'm going to need to get your fingerprints."

Well, not exactly what I wanted to do today, but I knew I wanted to be ruled out as a suspect so I complied.

CHAPTER FOUR

Two days later, Bella, Shadow, and I were back at work. Alexis didn't have any appointments, so she chose to stay at home with Joshua for one more day. It was certainly understandable that she wasn't as eager.

I continued Bella's training. She was a natural on the computer and had already updated our scheduling system with all the changes over the past twenty-four hours.

"Hello, Michelle," I said as my client walked in. "So good to see you today. I'm very sorry I had to reschedule—I hope it wasn't too inconvenient."

"That's okay, Libby, I understand. My husband said he thought he saw some police here the other evening on his way home from work?"

Darn! I was really hoping none of our clients would

learn about the police presence here—not good for business.

"Oh, yes, just a minor thing. All taken care of, no worries! Bella has you all checked in, go ahead and get changed and I'll join you in the Serenity room shortly."

Turning to Bella after Michelle exited the lobby, I said, "That reminds me, please don't talk about the incident with clients, ok? We need to keep this very quiet."

"Of course, Libby. No problem."

Michelle was a long-term client of ours now. A couple years back, she was the winner of our grand opening raffle and won a year's worth of massages. Of course, it was limited to one massage per month, but still, it was a great prize and she definitely took full advantage. I've been her therapist ever since. She's one of our clients who doesn't talk very much during her session, so I was quite surprised how chatty she was today.

"The graffiti came off the windows quite nicely— you'd never know. Was that why the police were here?"

"Yes, it did. And, yes, they are still investigating the incident." Technically, that was not a lie. They were. She did not need to know that there was yet another incident since the tagging.

"I actually started hiding the fact that I'm still coming here from my husband," she stated.

"Why?"

"I think he feels it's too indulgent. He doesn't understand how helpful this is for my arthritis. Men!" she said exasperated. "What he doesn't know won't hurt him."

"Well, don't go getting yourself in marital trouble," I

said with some levity. "Do you suppose he could benefit from massage? Maybe then he'd understand?"

"Oh, noooooo. He would never." The tension was palpable. Her warm energy shot up through the skin and onto my fingertips within seconds. My body started to heat up and I felt slightly woozy for a moment.

I didn't press any further on that topic; generally, when I get these types of feelings it means I'm just picking up on the clients' energy. I have had episodes where a client's energy causes me distress. It's easy to transfer energy with skin-on-skin contact, most therapists experience this, but I've also had cases where I've actually had visions … I suppose I hallucinated. It hasn't happened in several months and, honestly, I don't care to ever relive that again.

Once she had mentioned her husband, I remembered that he had befriended my sister, Jordan, several years back. I wondered if Michelle ever learned about that friendship? Jordan hadn't mentioned him in years either. I'll have to ask her the next time I see her. Ninety minutes later, this session was done. Thankfully, I was feeling better so I didn't question it any further.

Michelle made her way to our Serenity room, as we encourage our guests to do. She poured herself some India Spice tea and sat gazing at the tranquility fountain to relax. I headed up front to see what Bella and Shadow were up to. When I came through the frosted glass door to the front desk, I saw Shadow sleeping curled up at Bella's feet. Her head popped up when she heard me and she came wiggling her way over.

"Has she been out recently?" I asked Bella.

"It's probably about time. Would you like me to take her?"

"Nah, I need some fresh air. I'll take her over to the shady side of the building." Turning to Shadow in my sweet doggy-talk voice, I said, "Where's your leash? Wanna go outside?" Oh boy, did she! It was difficult to clasp her leash once she started the bouncy wiggles.

We followed the thin strip of shade along the sidewalk. Once we reached the shaded north end of the building, Shadow could do her business. I took several deep breaths realizing the air was hotter than what came out of my hair dryer this morning. Ugh. It's miserable. So much for a *fresh* breath of air.

"Boy, do I wish we could be in the mountains right now. Thirty degrees cooler—wouldn't that be nice?" I said, realizing that Shadow had no idea what I was talking about. She just wagged her tail.

On our way back, I saw JJ pull up to the building and get out of his car. He waved and waited for us.

"Hey, Libby!" he hollered to me. Once we approached him, his voice got sweet and he bent down to give Shadow an ear rub. "Oh, look at this good girl. She scares off the bad men, yeah … Shadow's a tough girl." She loved the attention; it certainly got her charged up.

"How is Alexis today?" I asked.

"She's doing well. I'm happy that she didn't have any appointments though." He still looked worried.

"Any progress on finding who might have been responsible for this?"

"I haven't heard anything, and I did stop by the desk to ask. I've been so wrapped up in this cold case that I'm not actually at the station much these days honestly."

"How's that going—the cold case? You promised to tell me more about it, but never got around to it with everything else that's happened. What's it about?"

"Murder. Dude killed his wife and three kids in 2006. Talk about brutal. Each was shot, and then he burned down the house. Actually, witnesses describe it more as an explosion. He hasn't been seen since. He and his dog, to be precise."

"Wow. That's horrible. What's he look like … who are we looking for?"

"He'd be around fifty-eight now. Gray hair. When this happened, it was cropped similar to mine. He's tall— around six foot two or three. Not a heavy guy, maybe two hundred pounds. Who knows though? In fifteen years, he could have long hair and be a huge fat guy for all we know."

"You said there have been some sightings though. Did they describe him?"

"Yeah, and they all describe him as being the same as when he went missing. That's the problem I'm having. People see an old photo and then suddenly every man looks like that person from a decade ago. They don't realize he's probably changed."

"Maybe he hasn't changed much?" I added.

"Perhaps. He was a military man and from everything I've read on the case, he's very regimented. He's a survivalist, too. Friends and family at the time said he could live off the land for a long time. Fifteen years long? I doubt it. Someone is helping him stay hidden—if he's alive at all."

We moved inside as we both started sweating. Bella was checking Michelle out and JJ followed me back to the offices.

"Lexi wanted me to pick up a box from her office. Then I'll be out of your hair," he said.

"You are never in our hair, JJ!" I ribbed him a little.

"Oh, I meant to ask you. Since you were an officer that regularly patrolled my mother's neighborhood, was there a lot of drug crime occurring over there."

"Oh, yeah. Definitely. And petty theft, too—probably the druggies stealing and selling to get money for their habit."

"Really? I thought that whole senior community was safe. Since when is it crime ridden?"

"What neighborhood is truly safe anymore, Libby? There's theft that occurs in nearly every area these days. It's up to the residents to keep their eyes open and report occurrences to help us get these thieves."

"Wow. I've been so naïve. And, more importantly, my mom is probably right."

"What's goin' on, Libby?"

"Well, I was over there the other day and she was obsessed with these kids—teens, maybe twenties?—riding their bikes through her neighborhood. Oh, and they had backpacks on."

"Yep, they load those packs with items they can easily get their hands on. They love to slip into a garage a resident has left open and grab as many tools as they can. It's been known that they'll search for an open window, watch the homeowner leave, and they'll sneak in and grab silverware and small objects. Seniors are the easiest targets."

I just stood there with my jaw dropped. When I watched the kids riding their bikes through the neighborhood—I never considered them actually being thieves. I just don't even think that way.

"Great. I need to apologize to my mom then. I just thought she doesn't have enough to do these days and she's making stuff up."

"No, she's very smart to keep her eyes open. She and her neighbors can start a neighborhood watch group and work with the police to catch them."

"I'll mention it to her. And, what you said about open garage and windows. I'm fairly sure she's good about staying locked up, but I'll double check."

"Hey, I gotta get going. Let me just grab that box," he said, as he stepped into the office and found what he was looking for. "I'll talk to you later, Libby!"

* * *

After a full day's work, I was ready to relax and unwind. You would think in my line of work, it's all about rest and relaxation. Well, it's not. Actually, it's quite the workout— not only for my hands and arms, but also for my legs and core. Standing all day and leaning in for the deep pressure maneuvers, I definitely feel it by the time I go home at night.

Shadow and I drove up to the house, parked in the garage, and then walked out to the mailbox. On the way back, approaching the house, I noticed she was suddenly on guard. Shadow heard something. The hackles raised along her back, her nose was pointed toward the side of my house, and her tail between her legs. She growled a real low guttural sound. I knew Bella wasn't home—she had school tonight and her car wasn't here. I listened for a moment and then moved for the front door with my key ready to insert into the lock. Of course, Shadow wasn't going to budge, so I just stretched out the leash as far as it would go and did a little one-leg dance and long-arm stretch to reach the lock.

"C'mon Shadow, you're not making this easy." She was continuing to pull me around the front of the house to the side yard. "Shadow! Let's go!" I said in a firm voice. I didn't want to get ambushed standing here.

She eventually acquiesced and we made our way in the front door where I quickly proceeded to lock it. Of course, she ran immediately to the back door, started jumping up and down, giving an excited bark. It wasn't the warning vocals, so she probably needed to go potty.

We walked outside and she took off toward the same side of the house where she was wanting to go from the front yard. I followed her. The daylight was quickly diminishing, but I could still see without a flashlight. When I rounded the corner of the house, she was standing up as though she wanted to look in my bedroom window. She looked at me approaching and I swear she tapped the very bottom of the window frame.

"What is it, girl?" I moved closer. She jumped down and then back up again, several times. When I saw exactly where her paw kept tapping, on the window's frame, I knew precisely what she was concerned about. First, it was evident that the window screen had been torn. As I inspected closer, the metal frame looked as though a tool had been used to pry the frame. It was bent upward and there were many scratches and indentations as though someone had been working at it.

Now that I was on the case, Shadow ran over to the gate and jumped on it. It flew open. *What the heck? It had a padlock on it, there's no way she should be able to push it open.* I ran after Shadow, but soon realized that she didn't get far. She was sniffing around the front of the house, just where it rounds to the front yard. Her nose was in a bush, and when

I looked closer, I saw there was a spray paint can, dangling among the bush's stems. I grabbed Shadow by the collar and got her back inside the backyard and latched the gate. We ran inside.

My pulse was racing. On the verge of panic, I grabbed my phone off the kitchen counter and called the police.

CHAPTER FIVE

All the doors were locked when I had arrived home. While I waited for the police and was still on with the emergency operator, I checked all the windows; none of them were broken or open. Nothing appeared to have been disturbed in the house either so I was confident no one actually broke in.

The police arrived within ten minutes and I showed them the tampered window that Shadow discovered. Officer Lahey agreed, someone had tried to pry the window open exactly as they'd seen in many of their burglary cases. What disturbed me most was the discovery that my padlock on the side gate had been cut. The police found it laying in the rocks. They took it and the spray paint can into evidence.

I realized then that I hadn't been paying attention.

"Uh, I'm sorry. I, er … what did you ask me?" My mind was foggy; something was nagging at me.

"You don't sleep with your windows open, do you?" she asked again.

"No. Not this time of year for sure." It rarely goes below the high eighties overnight during July. Who keeps their windows open?

"Good. Even when the weather cools, we advise to keep all doors and windows locked. Now, I have no idea if this was the rapist or a burglary attempt. No way to know yet. We've got the items we need to extract prints from, but many of these cases rarely get solved." She finished writing, closed her notepad, and moved to get up off the sofa.

It was then that I realized what was nagging at me. The spray paint can.

"I don't know if you are aware, but I own Dharma Inspired Day Spa. Last week we had a vandal that spray painted the front of our building. A couple days later, a man broke in and held my partner at gunpoint. My dog, Shadow, and I walked in and startled him so he ran off."

"I see where you're going with this. You are wondering if this occurrence here tonight at your home is connected with the incident at work?" she asked.

"Our business is right around the corner from here, not far at all," I added.

"Well, until we get these prints identified, it's hard to tell. Thank you for the added information though. Who was the officer on that case?" she asked, after scribbling the last-minute notes into her notepad.

"Um, Gonzales?" My brain was still not working well as I tried to recall. "Oh, and Talin."

"Sounds about right. I'll check in when I get back to

the precinct. In the meantime, Libby, keep your doors locked and keep your head up when you are out and about. Great dog, by the way … she's very sharp." Officer Lahey reached down to pet Shadow, who sat on my feet and never left my side. "She's just a pup, isn't she? How old?"

"Ah, yeah … she's my sweetheart. She's about nine months old. Time really flies, feels like I just got her."

"Well, you've done a great job with her training. She's very well behaved for an energetic pup."

"Thank you. I can't take all the credit though. I feel she pretty much came to me this way. Ok, well … we spend a lot of time together and maybe that's it. But, regardless, it's clear that we were made for each other." I smiled, got up off the couch, and walked the officer to the front door where she met up with another officer outside. He had just finished taking prints from around the window.

"Here's my card. Call me if anything else comes to mind."

Bella was coming up the walkway just as the officers turned to leave. I introduced them and they talked to her for a bit while I went back into the house. After several minutes, she came into the living room with a worried look on her face.

"Did they actually break in and steal anything?" she asked me.

"No, there's no evidence they actually got in the house. Thank God."

"I'm starting to get really worried, Libby. Someone is after you and Alexis. Maybe even me?"

Oh boy, I didn't want to trigger this girl any more than she already had been. It's only been a few months since her ordeal, growing up with a mother who completely traumatized her.

"Listen, Bella. I think these are just a few unfortunate events. That's all. I don't know what's going on in our world, but what I do know is that we have this girl," I turned to Shadow and fluffed up the fur on her neck, "and she's going to keep us safe."

"I can't believe she discovered that there was someone on the property! She is such a good girl ..." Bella rubbed her ears too. Shadow was loving every bit of the attention, and got so excited when Bella got up and opened the cookie jar. Not the people cookies, but Shadow's very own cookie jar, complete with her name on it.

We talked until around eleven and I realized I had never eaten dinner. That's what stress does, I guess. I had no appetite whatsoever; I only wanted sleep.

Once I had brushed my teeth and crawled into bed, I called Greg. I needed something to get my mind off the fact that my bedroom window had nearly been the entry point for a thief, at best, or a rapist in the worst-case scenario. Neither made me feel comfortable in my own home.

"Well, good evening, Miss Madsen. How are you?" he answered, with his smooth, calm voice that I had come to love. He calmed me and centered me.

"Hi! It's so good to hear your voice." He must have heard the hesitation in mine.

"Libby, what's wrong?" How on earth did he pick up on something being 'wrong'? He never ceased to amaze me. After all, it's not like we've been together for years—it's only been three months.

"I don't want to worry you, but yes, we've had more adventures around here—and not the kind of adventure I normally love."

"Go on…" he coaxed.

"Shadow discovered that someone tried to break into our house. Don't worry, they didn't succeed. We may have scared them off when we drove up. Not sure."

"What!? That's it, Libby. It's too dangerous down there in the city. You need to move up here to my small town." He sounded adamant. And, boy, his town is a *small* town. Not sure I'm quite ready for that, but I couldn't really disagree with the sentiment. The city does seem to be more dangerous all the time.

"Ok, well, let's not get too far out in front of our headlights, mister." I laughed it off and proceeded to tell the details I knew. He agreed that the spray paint can seemed to indicate there might be something related to the spa incident. After a few minutes, hashing through those details, I let him know that I really wanted to talk about anything else—so I could have any chance of sleeping tonight.

We dreamed of the day that the forest fires would be out, the pandemic would settle down, and perhaps a time where we could take his RV and go on a fun adventure together. At the moment, that seemed impossible, but we were holding steadfast to the belief that our world would get better soon.

CHAPTER SIX

It was Monday morning, four full days since she was traumatized at the spa, when Alexis walked back through the front door. Bella greeted her warmly and I poured her a nice hot cup of Ashwagandha tea.

"It's so nice to have you back, we missed you!" I said, as I handed her the cup of tea. She set her purse in her desk drawer and plugged in her laptop to the docking station.

"You know, it feels good to be back." She looked around the office and then her loving smile spread across her face. "Yes, it is time to move on and get back into the swing of things!"

With that, we both set out to get ready for our sessions—it was going to be a busy day.

I nearly ran into Bella coming through the doors to the

lobby.

"Look what Michelle just dropped by!" Bella exclaimed. "Freshly baked scones. There's blueberry, cinnamon, and cranberry-orange. I'm going to set them out in the relaxation room—these will be fantastic with our selection of teas."

"Wow, she's ambitious. That's very thoughtful of her."

"She said she baked five dozen—both for her church and for us."

"Again, *very* ambitious. I can't even remember the last time I baked." Seriously, I do basic cooking and my InstaPot is my best friend for that. Baking—well, that usually comes from a box. As long as I only have to add an egg, oil, and water, we're good. Otherwise, I just purchase from the grocery store's bakery and call it good.

"Yes, she's very thoughtful. I worry about her though."

"How so?"

"Have you met her husband before?"

"I may have a couple years back, at the grand opening, but I really don't recall anything about him." I wasn't going to mention Jordan's connection to him since it turned out to be benign. It was true, I didn't know him.

"It's just some of the things she talks about when she's here. Today, she was admiring my nail polish." Bella spread out her fingers, displaying her hot pink gel manicure. "Then she proceeded to tell me her husband would never *allow* her to wear that bright of a color. Can you imagine?"

"Really? No, I cannot imagine Greg *ever* telling me anything like that. Well, we wouldn't be dating if he did because what business it is of his what color goes on *my nails*?"

"Exactly. Of course, maybe I'm overly sensitive. It

brings back the controlling ways of my mother…" Bella's voice softened. "I have to remember so many people lead lives the rest of us never see. I think that is why I worry about Michelle."

I gave Bella a hug. "I can definitely see that. You may see something in her that reminds you of everything you've been through. I hope he's not really *that* bad. Maybe she's just sensitive to the fact that he doesn't like the color and she chooses not to wear it?"

"Maybe. I guess. I just don't like an adult woman referring to something her husband doesn't 'allow'."

"True. That's odd. Oh hey, I've gotta get ready for my ten o'clock." I headed back to the massage rooms.

* * *

Not long after I'd finished my lunch, Alexis was finished with her client and joined me in our office. After listening to her voice mail, she turned to me.

"JJ is in Ohio for a couple days on his case. Wanna join me and Joshua for dinner tonight? Bella, too, if she's not already doing anything."

"That sounds perfect. I'd love to. I'll see what she's up to tonight. What time?"

"I think we're finished here around five, looking at the schedule. How about six? And, you know Shadow is always included in any invite, too, right?" She took her eyes off her computer and looked up for my answer.

"We'll be there!" I smiled, put away my lunch containers into the insulated bag I brought, then headed up to the front desk. On the way, I stopped in the locker rooms just to be sure everything was clean for our next clients. Bella does a great job of cleaning, but I know she's had her hands full at the front desk so I try to also help out on occasion.

"Hey there, Libby!" Alexis' long-time client and neighbor was at the sink washing her hands. Anytime I see Sasha Adams, it makes me want to go grab a hair brush and maybe dab on some makeup. She is a model and *always* looks perfect.

"Hi Sasha!" I moved to give her a hug. We both were masked, but in this new crazy pandemic world we live in, there's always that hesitation whether you *should* give someone a hug. It's not like we ever thought about this before the killer virus struck. After the slightest hesitation, she met me for the hug and we embraced. "It's so good to see you again, it's been awhile, hasn't it?"

"It has. I don't even know why … it's not like I've been traveling this year. I'm not sure why I haven't spent all my time here with Alexis getting pampered or joining her meditations."

"Well, we were closed for a couple months. It's good to be back open. I don't think she's held a group meditation session since we reopened. Anyway, great to see you … enjoy your massage!"

I finished wiping down the high-touch areas and proceeded to the front desk. Isobel was chatting with my next client, who just so happened to also be my mother, Julia.

"Hello, Mother," I squirted hand sanitizer in my palm and rubbed my hands together. "Ready for your session?"

"Boy, am I!" She followed me back through the locker rooms. "You see, right here around my shoulder is really stiff. I think I slept on it wrong. My whole neck hurts."

"Ok, get changed here. Grab a robe and then I'll meet

you in the Serenity room." I blew her a kiss and moved through the door as she started to change her clothes.

Bella had already beat me back to the massage rooms and nearly had the table dressed with new clean sheets when I walked in. Shadow was following her … yes, just like a shadow. These two had a special connection, that was very evident.

During my mother's massage, I learned all about the new goings on in her community. The house we are now referring to as the 'drug house' had been seeing a lot of activity. Young people are coming and going all times of the day and night. Several times the sheriff's deputies have been over there. She wasn't sure if anything meaningful happened—didn't see them hauled off in handcuffs or anything.

"Margie and I want to get a watch group put together. I think Doreen is all for it too. Do you think JJ can come over and talk to my neighbors about that?"

"Mom, JJ doesn't really do that in the police department. He is actually working on a cold case with a group of detectives. Might be up for a promotion soon. I'm sure if you call the local precinct, they can get you in touch with the right person."

"Oh, I really wanted JJ to do it. I trust him," she whined.

"Well, let's see … I'm sure JJ would be perfectly willing to talk with you and Margie about your concerns when he gets back from Ohio."

"What's he doing in Ohio?" she sounded perturbed.

"I just told you, Mom … he's working on a cold case." Trying to stay patient, I put on my calmest voice. "He'll be back in a few days, I think."

"Ohhh. Didn't realize he left the state."

"Well, even when he gets back, he's very busy with this case so it's probably best to call the police station, see what you can get going, then talk to JJ whenever he gets home— if it makes you feel better."

"Those kids are making all my neighbors very nervous. It's like a gang of 'em. I heard through Margie that Stan down the street thinks they broke into their house and stole some valuables while they were gone."

"Did they report it to the police?" I asked

"I'm sure they did."

"Ok, then it will get sorted. Just make sure you always lock your doors and windows—even when you're home, not just when you leave the house."

"Oh, I do! Your dad got me in that habit years ago."

She settled into her massage after that and was quiet again until I had her turn over onto her back. Then she started up with my favorite subject.

"Meet a handsome man yet?" she asked me.

Doing my best to not sigh out loud, I just stated, "I've met lots of handsome men."

I decided when I met Greg that I was *not* going to introduce him or speak about him to her until a couple things happened; a) I knew he'd be around for a while, and b) I knew he could handle her badgering without giving into it or feeling sorry for me. Last thing I needed was Greg running back to the hills because Julia scared him away. Or, worse … a pity proposal to shut her up!

"Well, you know, Jordan has lots of friends and has said she'd set you up…"

I interrupted quickly, "NO! Mom, please… no!"

"Wow, you are so touchy, Libby. We're just trying to help. Both Jordan and I are concerned about you."

Oh, now Jordan is concerned, too? Right.

"Mom, please. When the time is right, it will happen. Can't you just leave this alone?" I pleaded.

I've got to reconsider offering massages to my mother ... this is unbearable, being literally locked in a room with her.

* * *

Bella accepted the invitation to the Johnson's that evening. She, Shadow, and I loaded up in Trina, my 4Runner, and we headed the short five miles to their house. Yes, you may or may not know this about me yet, but I do name my vehicles. I pretty much name most animate or inanimate objects. For instance, I've named some of my plants and trees in my garden ... the moringas are aptly named "Morrie" and a mesquite I've named "Missy." Another large tree on my side yard is a Tipu that I've named "Tippy". I know, I know ... I didn't say that I was super creative in the naming business. How Trina got her name? Well, the sales lady at the Toyota dealership was very nice, we became fast friends, and her name was Trina ... voila, Trina the Toyota!

Alexis already had the margaritas blended and poured when we walked into her kitchen. Strawberry tonight—she explained there was a good sale at Sprouts.

"Fresh *homemade* strawberry margaritas—not the flavored bottle mixtures?" I marveled as I took a sip. "This is delicious!"

Bella gave a hearty agreeable nod as she took another big sip and then grimaced when the cold went straight to her head.

Alexis must have seen my eyes widen as I stared at

the *huge* pitcher full of the yummy pink juice. "I invited Sasha from next door also, but she declined. She's been very secluded since the pandemic started—other than her massage today, she explained she just isn't getting out much."

"Oh well, probably best that we don't have others outside of our little bubble … unless we wanted to manage margarita sipping around masks." I laughed as I watched Alexis check the oven.

"What are we having tonight? It smells terrific in here," I asked.

"I have roasted veggies—beets, sweet potato, and onion—in here." She closed the upper oven door. "Then we'll put those over a bed of spinach, carrot, and pumpkin seeds. And in the lower oven is the teriyaki marinated chicken."

Bella dipped a spoon into the glaze for a taste test. "Oh wow, *that* is amazing!"

"Hey, where's Joshua?" I asked.

"You know, he wore himself out today. Swimming and being spoiled by the sitter—which probably means too much sugar and no afternoon nap. He's out like a light."

"Oh, I'll miss that sweet boy." Bella looked sad.

Alexis put on some smooth R&B quietly in the background and we moved to sit on the plush gray U-shaped sectional sofa in the center of the family room. Everything about Alexis' environment was soft, muted, and stunningly beautiful. How she keeps it this way with a small boy running around constantly, I'll never understand. She is your modern super mom for sure. Works full-time and parents fully too. Of course, she has the luxury of setting her own schedule, but she is one who stays constantly busy, yet remains so calm and centered.

"Anything from the police yet related to your property damage?" she asked me.

"No, I need to follow up with Office Lahey or Talin, I suppose." I shrugged and rolled my eyes. "I don't think we're going to hear much about either case. I get the sense they're just seeing it as petty and they have larger stuff to figure out."

Bella piped up, "Alexis being held at gunpoint is not petty!"

"Oh, I one hundred percent agree! Don't get me wrong. I just don't think they connect these incidents together." I took another swallow of my margarita. "None of us know if they're linked, but don't you think it's extremely odd where two crimes happen at the spa—and then someone tried to break into my home? And, spray paint at my house—and we're tagged at the spa? Coincidence?"

"I've thought the same—all these have to be the same person. Someone with a vendetta," Bella said looking at Alexis, remembering how she told us that the gunman said something similar to that.

Alexis got up off the couch effortlessly and glided across the floor—or, at least that's how it looked when her flowing long tunic floated behind her gracefully. The oven timer went off and she removed the veggies. Ten more minutes on the chicken.

Lexi turned to us. "The world has gone a little bit nutty lately and there are a lot of strange events going on. That we cannot deny. However, if they are all related, or specifically meant for us, we just don't know."

"True. I just wish it felt like the police took it more seriously. I want to find this perpetrator ... or perpetrators.

It's not right when someone can terrorize you and get away with it," I said with tears in my eyes. "No one is going to get away with harming my friend!"

"Hey, hey, hey…" Alexis moved across the room to sit next to me. Her hand softly touched my face, wiping the falling tear, "I'm fine. Believe that." Then, looking at both of us pointedly, she said, "Listen, you two, we are going to get through all this and the police *will* learn more. In the meantime, we are not going to sit here and feel sorry for ourselves or cry. We are going to get our girl-power on, sip these margaritas, maybe dance around the room, and then we'll eat a nutritious meal!" We all laughed at that, and Shadow must have understood something about dancing because she got up, wiggling and twisting all over. I wiped my tears, gave Lexi a huge hug, and we all started to dance.

Soon after, we set the table and sat down to enjoy a very nice meal. Shadow fell asleep at my feet; she was pooped out after tearing up the dance floor. The rest of the evening we laughed and talked only about the positive stuff in our lives.

On the way home, I felt better than I had in days. It was so energizing to be around friends that uplift. Alexis' energy is invaluable. *But, even so, I just don't think the police are doing enough right now.* I felt inspired from Alexis' speech and thought it was about time I did something to help them. If Alexis can overcome the horror of her personal safety being violated, I can certainly start nosing around to try and solve this.

Just as that warmth of remembering Alexis' strength and determination was flowing through me, we rounded the corner and pulled up to my house. There were several neighbors standing around talking outside on my front sidewalk. I will admit, it was slightly unnerving to see approximately ten people, all masked, standing right in front of the house. We put our masks on, leashed Shadow, and walked over to them.

"Everything alright?" I asked as we approached.

Ted, my neighbor who lives to the east of me, stepped forward. "Hi Libby! We were all just concerned about you."

"Why?"

"The police have interviewed quite a few of us—at least, those that live on either side, and in front and behind your house. What happened?"

I addressed the whole group. "Hi everyone. Good to see you—it's been a while. Look, it appears there was a break-in attempt at my home last week. To be clear, whoever it was didn't succeed. We are fine." I pointed my hand toward Bella, to indicate all who live in the household.

"I heard there was some police activity over at your spa, too, is that true?" Mary, who lived on the other side of me, asked.

"Yes, we had an incident there, too."

A couple ladies turned and walked off muttering something about massage, along with their disapproving looks.

Ok, that was weird. Do I even know them?

Shaking off my thoughts about the rude women, I continued, "I'm sorry if these things have made some feel uneasy. I certainly don't want to be the center of any crime in our community. The police are looking into this and I'm sure they'll get to the bottom of it." I tried to reassure, but there were several skeptical expressions I saw on my neighbors' faces.

"Do you think it was that rapist?" Another man I

didn't recognize asked. "The police have asked for our security camera footage. I have a teenage girl and my wife to protect so, of course, I'm gravely concerned."

They all took turns speaking about their fears and speculation on what this world is coming to. As I stood and listened to each, I began to wonder why they seemed to think I would have the answers. Yes, Alexis and I were victims of crime, and yes, *maybe* Bella or I could have been the rapists' latest victims. It was as though this group was looking to me for answers to quell their fears. My earlier energetic and positive feelings were waning now. I found myself questioning what I could do about this situation. It also further inspired me to action.

That's it … I've got to figure out who is behind all this.

CHAPTER SEVEN

Greg and I talked on the phone the next morning before we both had to head off to work. One of the fires was nearly contained, but they were still fighting two others in the region. Firefighters were now fighting fatigue and they were bringing in reserves from New Mexico, Colorado, and Utah. The exhaustion was evident in Greg's voice as well. This had gone on now for nearly four weeks.

"I will get a few days off toward the end of the week, I was thinking of coming down to the city." He suddenly sounded giddy, but then paused and added, "If that's okay with you?"

I could hardly control my excitement. "Of course, it's okay with me! I would love to see you in person; this phone call stuff is getting super old."

"I agree. I need a hug about now." His voiced cracked a tiny bit and I nearly lost it.

"We both do, sweetie, and we'll spend a few days trying not to think about the tough stuff going on right now.

We talked for a few more minutes and then both went about our days.

I drove over to my mom's house around lunchtime, after my morning appointment. Jordan was coming over to join us for lunch. As I walked in her house, I was happy to see she didn't bring all the children. I was still of the opinion that until the vaccine is available, our mom should not interact directly with them. We all agreed to wear our masks while we were indoors visiting.

"Jordan, hello," I greeted, giving her a quick hug.

"Libs—how are things at the spa? I guess more to the point, how's Alexis doing?"

"Surprisingly, she's handling everything great. I just wish the police were doing more."

My mom spoke up. "The police just can't handle all they're dealing with these days. We've decided in this neighborhood, we're going to take things into our own hands." She did a little fist pump and both Jordan and I busted out laughing. This new 'senior spirit' was by far the funniest thing I've ever seen my mother do.

"So, you called and got the Neighborhood Watch officers to come speak to your community?" I asked.

"Yep. Margie and I are heading up the committee and we're taking back our neighborhood."

"I guess I must be out of the loop—what are you trying to stop?" Jordan asked us.

We started to move toward the kitchen while Mom explained all about the punks with backpacks. As they talked, I put together ham sandwiches and pilfered her pantry for some chips to go along. As I set their plates in front of them, I realized I'd tuned out most of their discussion until that moment and wondered what Mom was talking about now.

"...yes, the neighbor indicated they are putting in a gate. Right through my fence! So they can swim in my pool." Leaving both of her daughters staring with mouths gaping open, she dug right into her sandwich as though we were having a perfectly normal conversation.

"Mom, that's crazy. Certainly, that's not their intention." I had no idea where this latest news was coming from and how we got off the subject about the punks in the neighborhood. My mom's hearing is not what it used to be, but certainly, it also wasn't *that bad*. Did the neighbor really say those words? "You know it's illegal for them to access your backyard and use your pool without your permission, right?"

"Well, that's what he told me. That's what's happening." She was curt and very sure of her convictions.

"Is this George—who's lived there forever?" I asked.

"Yep. I think a family member moved in recently, don't know him, but started seeing him around starting just a few months back."

Jordan and I stared at one another for a second. Then she turned to Mom, "Ok. Ok, we will go talk to the neighbors. We'll make sure they know it's illegal and if they do anything of the sort, we'll call the police."

"The police won't do anything. Didn't you just hear me? We have to be vigilantes and take back our neighborhood from the punks. They aren't going to care whether neighbors are using my pool!"

Wow, I was literally frozen in place wondering what alternate world I had just stepped into. This didn't sound like my mother—why all doomsday all of a sudden? Neither of us knew what we could say that would improve the conversation, so we just quietly ate the rest of our lunch.

With just one knowing look between sisters, Jordan and I had the same thought, distract her with ice cream. I cleared the sandwich plates and my sister dug the ice cream out of the freezer and started dishing into small bowls. It was also silently understood that we would change the subject. Jordan spent the rest of our time together talking about her kids and pulling out her phone to show mom all the recent pictures.

I wanted to know more about the backpack bike-riding kids and, of course, I was chomping at the bit to talk to the neighbor. But, I sat and listened as she told all about Apple and Annie and their latest challenges with remote learning. Chase and Ryan are younger and not struggling with that, but they're pestering their sisters like crazy and Jordan is going out of her mind. Yes, it really makes me want to settle down and have a thousand kids, I was thinking sarcastically.

Finally, we were able to bail and head over to the neighbor's house. Jordan and I knocked on the door, but there was no one at home. I left a note tucked into their screen door asking for someone to call me when they had a chance.

After hugging my sister and saying goodbye, I drove around the neighborhood looking for suspicious activity. Today must be a slow day because I didn't spot even one bicyclist. However, just as I turned another corner, I saw a very scantily clad young woman walking my direction in the street, just off the sidewalk. She definitely didn't look like she belonged in this neighborhood. Long black hair down past her behind, super skinny, but with an hour-glass shape highlighting her slightly wider torso and hips than waist. I slowed down, pulling over slightly, and rolling down my window. I stared at her heavily rouged cheeks and spider-like black eyelashes. It was hard *not* to stare.

Spontaneously, I decided to put on an act. In a high-toned voice, I tried making a connection with the girl. "Heyyy, I'm supposed to meet … oh, uh, what's his name?" I pretended to look for something on my passenger seat. "He's got *something* for me," I winked.

"He's late." Her hand landed on her left hip at the exact moment her right hip thrust out in an almost unnatural pose. She smacked her gum, blew a huge bubble, and sucked it back into her bright red-lipped mouth. "Or, you're too early. They're not usually this side 'til after three."

I stumbled for a moment; I was so surprised she hadn't completely blown me off and kept walking. Slumping down into my seat, trying to be cool, I lowered my voice even more, and softened my eyes. "Oh. Hey, uh, like, I can't remember … well, he told me his name. What is it again?"

"Lanky."

I nearly choked and struggled to hold back the laughter that was bubbling up. Really? Lanky? "Right. Right. That's it. *Lanky.*" I exaggerated, snapping my fingers at the same time. "So, I s'pose he's still over at…uh, you know…"

"Yeah, he's with Big K. You can find him over there." She blew another bubble and it popped leaving an oblong pink shape stuck over her mouth and part of her cheeks until she pulled it off with her fingers and shoved it back in her mouth.

"Ah, yep ... definitely remember Big K. We're tight. Where's his crib?" *I really don't know where those words came from...*

Her eyes squinted and the corner of her mouth turned up. Definitely, there were jealous vibes before she answered, "Extension. Broadway."

"Oh, right. Right. I'll catch up with them there. Thanks!" I moved to roll the window up and she stopped me by putting her hand on the frame.

"I did you one, now you do me one," she moved her face lower into the window and held her hand out.

I just wanted her face away from mine as she was popping bubbles. Luckily, I had a twenty in my shorts pocket and didn't have to reach into my purse. I pulled it out and gave it to her. I also gave her a bottle of water—it was awfully hot out and I couldn't imagine walking in this heat. She must have been satisfied with that because she tucked the cash in between her very large bosom, presumably in her bra, and then turned to continue her walk down the street and taking a sip from the water bottle.

I'm not entirely sure what all I've learned here. There's a Lanky, a Big K, and what looks to be a prostitute strolling down the street in a senior living community. I think it is safe to say that Lanky and Big K are drug dealers. Even if I didn't overtly ask for drugs, it was certainly implied. She was definitely selling something entirely different altogether. And, does any of this have anything to do with what's happening just a few miles up the road in my neighborhood? I have no idea if it ties together, but nevertheless, I am concerned about my mother's well-being now. Oh, and I know that 'Lanky' hangs out after three in this area. Perhaps Shadow and I should take our evening walk in this neighborhood.

When I got back to the spa, Bella and Shadow were at the front desk. Alexis was in a session with her client. Shadow came bounding over to me and soaked up all the love I gave her. It was obvious she enjoyed being a fixture now at our workplace.

"Your two o'clock cancelled. And, now you have a session scheduled at four. Hope that's okay?"

"Yes, definitely. Why did Sage cancel?"

"She's not feeling stellar. Said she was going to play it safe."

"Ok, yes … I love when clients consider others. Cancellations are a blessing in this climate now."

"Oh, and I was hoping to take off a little earlier today for school? Maybe by three, if that's okay with you?

"Sure, that's not a problem."

"Alexis won't be out of her session when I leave. Can you make sure she checks her desk for messages? JJ called earlier hoping to catch her. He'll be back tomorrow morning instead of tonight. She needs to get Joshua from the sitter."

"Will do."

I really wanted to talk to JJ myself, but I wouldn't bother him on the job. I could wait until he returned tomorrow. Since he used to patrol Mom's area, I was hoping he could give me some intel on these new characters I'd just learned about.

Once Bella left for the day, I sat at the front desk to

check out Alexis' clients and then ultimately, to greet my own four o'clock client. I checked our schedules for the next couple weeks. With Greg coming to town, I wanted to make sure my calendar was updated so I could spend some quality time with him.

The door chimed, I looked up to find Michelle coming in with more treats. This time it looked like cupcakes.

"Hi Libby." Her voice didn't sound as upbeat and bubbly as usual. "Do you have a moment?"

"Sure. What's up? Seems serious?"

Her voice cracked as she started to speak. "I'm sorry. I have to cancel my membership here." Her face flushed and she was visibly upset.

"Ok. We can certainly do that. But, can you share why?" I asked, as I guided her to a nearby chair so we could sit down.

"First, these are for you gals." She handed me the plate of eight beautifully decorated cupcakes.

"Thank you. They look delicious!" I exclaimed. "Now, what is going on? Did we do something wrong? Is it the recent police activity here that has scared you?"

She smiled. "No, no … nothing like that. It's just … well, my husband. I think I told you I was sneaking around to keep coming here?"

"Yes. You did."

"Well, he figured it out. I can't keep lying to my husband."

"No, you shouldn't have to," I stated.

"I know. I know. I was doing it to keep the peace. I *love* coming here, Libby. This is the brightest spot in my day … it's so relaxing and I truly feel better after every time I've been here." She sniffled, took a tissue out of her purse, removed her mask and wiped her nose. "He believes it's sinful."

"Sinful?" Seems extreme, but I wanted to learn more. "What exactly is the sin?"

"I don't know. I mean, we are good church-going folks and live respectable lives. I don't feel I'm doing anything wrong. Apparently, he believes that all massage places are sex businesses."

"Oh, that's just ridiculous, Michelle! Have you ever felt unsafe?"

"No, no, Libby. Never. You are wonderful and the two of you have built a fantastic business here. My husband … well, let's just say he has a lot of opinions on many topics. This is just one of them." She quivered and her eyes lowered.

"Michelle, I have to ask you. Are you safe at home?"

She hesitated for a good minute or two. Then slowly, carefully, she raised her eyes to meet mine. "My husband has had a very difficult life. Most of it when he was younger—but, there were things done to him that have affected him deeply. I knew he wasn't a perfect man when I met him. I mean, none of us are perfect, are we? We all make mistakes, and we all make sacrifices." Her hand was shaking as she lifted it and performed the holy trinity, then continued, "But, Libby, he has taken good care of me. I have a good home and he provides very well for us. I know I have to make concessions to keep a happy marriage, and this is one of them."

I realized she never answered my question whether she was safe, but I felt if I pushed too hard, she would only shut down more. I kept her talking for a short time, offering her tea and a cupcake. She shared a lot with me. I felt sad for her. My intuition told me that there was much more she wasn't telling me. But, at the end of the day, if she chose to have an overbearing and controlling husband, that was her business. I just prayed he wasn't actually mentally or physically harming her. It's amazing how we, as massage therapists, come to know our clients and feel as though they are somehow part of our friend or family group. Alexis has shared the same sentiment with me as well, so I know we become affected when any one of our clients are going through difficult times. For now, I had to let this one go. I gave her a friendly hug goodbye, secretly praying for her well-being.

CHAPTER EIGHT

It had been over a month since we'd seen each other and I was getting that excited feeling in the pit of my stomach as I waited for his gray Tundra to pull up into my driveway. Before the handsome forest ranger came into my life, I really wasn't looking to date—much to my mother's chagrin, of course. I'm perfectly fine heading off, just me and my dog, to go camping, hiking, or really, traveling anywhere. In fact, there are times I actually prefer it. However, since meeting Greg Lawson, all of that has changed. I constantly think of *my* adventures now as *ours*. This year's fire season in Arizona has been a particularly awful one and it has prevented us from seeking outdoor adventure as much as we'd like. For one, he has to work overtime. And also, the forests where we would normally find ourselves traipsing through are closed.

Shadow detected the truck in the driveway before I heard anything. She was barking and jumping up and down at the front door. Even though Greg now had his own key—given after an incident a few months ago when he saved my life—I opened the door, allowing Shadow to greet him first so she wouldn't bowl me over.

Greg had his hands full with a couple duffel bags, but he set them down on the concrete and kneeled down alongside Shadow to shower her with all his love. Standing back and watching, I saw that Shadow clearly loved this kind, gentle man. He stood, leaving his bags where they were, and stepped over to me. His hands slipped around my mid-section and he pulled me close into a full embrace, and planted a huge kiss on my lips. Shadow sat staring at us, but I could feel her wiggles and squirming, ready to pounce any second for some more attention.

We laughed as we walked inside with her still bouncing everywhere. He put his bags in my room and then we joined together in the kitchen for some coffee.

"You had to have gotten up pretty darn early, Mr. Lawson, to be here by nine," I teased.

"Ok, busted. I was excited to get here as soon as I could."

"Well, as you can tell, both Shadow and I were also excited for you to get here. Want some breakfast?"

"Whatcha thinking?"

"Breakfast burritos? I make a mean bacon, egg, potato, with yummy green chile sauce and melted cheese…"

"Sold!"

I started to get out the ingredients for the burritos. He gave in to Shadow's pestering and took her outside to the backyard. When they came in again, he mentioned the bedroom window.

"I see where they tried to get in. Libby, why don't you have cameras?"

"I don't know. I guess I've always felt I lived in a good neighborhood and this type of thing doesn't happen here. Guess I'm wrong."

"Well, while I'm here, let's take care of that, ok?"

"*That's* what you want to spend your time doing?" I said, teasingly.

"Ok, maybe not *all my time*."

"That would be very sweet of you to help me with that. I'm not great at those electronic things. Oh, and maybe we could get some cameras for my mom's house, too?" I suggested.

"Of course. That means I get to meet her?" His eyebrows shot up.

Horrified, I realized what I just did. No, he can't meet my mom.

"Uh. You're not ready for that yet. Maybe I'll just pay attention to how you set mine up, then I'll deal with my mom's later."

"You really don't want me to meet her, do you?"

"Oh, trust me, it's not you. It's not even you and me. You just don't know what kind of pestering we will get for eternity if I introduce you now. She's relentless and she'll have us married off in no time." I realized at that second, I probably shouldn't have brought that up.

"Married?" he teased.

"Well, you know … she thinks I'm a spinster in my late thirties and not married. That's all. I don't want her getting ahead of herself and badgering *you* over *her* fixation."

He laughed, came up behind me at the stove and wrapped his arms around my waist. "Whenever you are ready, I'm ready for Ms. Julia Madsen. Don't worry." I turned my head for a kiss and then got back to the bacon. *Will I ever be ready for that?*

"I think I'll keep you to myself for a little longer—I'm selfish that way."

"Hey, where's Bella this morning?" he asked.

"She and Alexis are already at work. I cleared my schedule for a couple days. Only one massage had to be adjusted—and that client loves Alexis so it was no problem."

"You haven't said in a while how Bella is doing."

"Oh, I think she's really doing well. I can't wait for you to see her … I think you'll agree she's a totally different girl than just a few months ago when we found her." It was cute how much father-like concern Greg had displayed since his instrumental part in her missing person's case.

"It sounds like she has settled in at the spa, and school too. That's a lot for anyone to take on so soon."

"That's what I told her, too. She's handling it all brilliantly. I think staying busy keeps her mind from going back there." I finished folding the large tortillas to wrap all the ingredients inside, then covered them in green chile sauce and shredded sharp cheddar cheese. My stomach was growling. "Ok, grab another cup of coffee if you'd like; these are ready," I said as I set a huge plate of smothered burrito down in front of him.

"Oh my, this looks fantastic!"

We both settled in to eating breakfast and planning out our few days together. Since most entertainment type venues were closed due to the pandemic, it wasn't like we could really go 'out' but we came up with several creative things we'd like to do: very early morning hikes, install those cameras, get together with the Johnsons, and with the little eyebrow wiggle, he suggested some private time activities, too.

"Alexis mentioned yesterday that they wanted us to come over for movie night. I think that's for tonight? They have a nice outdoor setup in their backyard."

"Ohhh, outdoor movies, that does sound fun!"

"I'll get more details later, but yeah, sounds fun to me too."

* * *

Bella had school work to do and decided to opt-out of movie night, so it was just us two couples and Shadow, after Joshua went to bed that night.

JJ walked in from the backyard. "Everything is set up. Still want to watch the movie from the pool or should I set up chairs on the deck?"

"Pool!" Greg was first to answer. "I think I'll melt out there. I don't know how y'all handle this heat."

I started laughing. I always forget that even though Greg has lived in Arizona for a long time, he is *not* accustomed to our heat in the valley. He lives at seven thousand feet in elevation and although it can routinely get into the nineties in Heber, it also cools way down overnight. Many nights in the Phoenix metro area never get below ninety as the *low* temperature during the height of summer.

While we changed into our suits, Alexis whipped up another batch of mango margaritas and we all moved out to their beautiful backyard.

The space was not large, but their expertly done landscape transformed it into a beautiful tropical oasis. There were several varieties of palms, small to very large. They had desert drought-resistant mesquites and palo verde trees planted along the perimeter that enhanced overall shade in the yard, as well as privacy from neighbors. There was a small waterfall that flowed into a couple small ponds on either side of the pool for an added water feature. A built-in hot tub sat slightly higher and stair-stepped down into the pool.

JJ had set up the movie screen—a large white sheet over the edge of a pergola that sat at the far end of the pool—and a projector already. An impressive surround sound system finished the movie night set up. Once everyone was settled with their drinks at the pool's edge, JJ fired up the projector connected to his laptop. Earlier, we had agreed on watching *Knives Out*, a funny mystery that we hadn't seen yet. We had all changed into our suits and then climbed into the pool.

"Shadow! No, you can't get in the pool." She looked dejected, but went about patrolling the backyard.

"Okay, this is the only way to be outdoors in Phoenix in late July," Greg said as he took a sip of his drink. "So refreshing! Is it true that people actually *cool* their pools here?"

"It is true," JJ stated. "We didn't opt for that. Can you imagine the cost to literally air condition your pool in the summertime?"

We all settled into the movie and were dying laughing at the antics of these fantastic actors. I wasn't sure if I was just getting tipsy or what, but it seemed as though I just couldn't stop laughing. At least, it was all fun and games until our attention was abruptly distracted from the movie.

Shadow jumped up, barking from her place on the patio and ran to the wall.

"What was that sound?" Alexis said with alarm, already getting out of the pool. Drying off, she ran into the house.

JJ grabbed for the projector's remote and paused the movie, then he also got out of the pool and followed Alexis into the house.

Greg and I sat staring toward their side yard at the west end of the house, listening to see if we heard it again. I noticed lights on in both houses on either side so it appeared people were home, but there didn't appear to be movement or any noises coming from the homes.

"Shadow! Quiet!" She stopped and came to the side of the pool. I petted her, holding her collar to keep her near. "We all heard it, didn't we?" I asked Greg. "Was it a scream?"

Greg shook his head. "I'm not sure what it was. So hard to know with the movie playing, huh?"

Alexis and JJ returned.

"Did you all hear it too?" JJ asked and we both nodded. "Shadow was definitely alerted to something."

"Well, everything is quiet in the house and Joshua is fast asleep. It wasn't him," Alexis informed.

Shadow settled down and our friends joined us back in the pool. We all had that nervous laughter as we settled back in, but decided we must be hearing things.

Just as JJ lifted the remote to start the movie again, we all heard a shrill sound. A woman's scream and then Shadow's barking. This time we all left the pool and dried off, wrapping our towels around us.

Greg and JJ headed to the side gate where they thought

the sound came from. Alexis and I moved under the patio cover, shuffling Shadow to come along with us. We paused to listen for any further noises. It was silent now, only the faint sound of traffic from a few blocks away.

* * *

"I don't see anything, do you?" Greg asked quietly. They both walked along the sidewalk past several houses on either side of the Johnson's.

"Seems very quiet in the neighborhood tonight, actually," JJ whispered as they continued along the sidewalk.

"Maybe the movie is making us a bit jumpy? Or, was it the sounds coming from the movie itself?"

"Shadow definitely heard something. I think we all heard it even after I shut off the movie? I thought it was a woman screaming, is that what it sounded like to you?"

"Yep, exactly."

JJ stopped, looked up and down the street. Confused, he shook his head. "Well, let's go back … nothing to see here."

They continued to the side of his house, rounded the corner, and entered the backyard through the side gate they had exited. Shadow barked.

* * *

Alexis and I startled when the two dark shadows appeared from behind a cluster of palms near the end of the covered patio. We quickly realized it was just the guys and our pulses settled down. I let go of Shadow and she ran to them.

The guys indicated they found nothing.

"Ok, so are we all jumpy or what?" Alexis laughed.

"Let's finish this movie!"

After laughing it all off, we agreed we wanted to finish the movie … we climbed back in the pool and had an amazing time floating around and laughing at the silly antics in the film. We heard nothing else and forgot all about it by the time the movie was over and we crawled out of the pool for the final time. It was nearly eleven and we sat around talking for another hour. Greg was interested in JJ's new case and his recent trip. We all learned more about the suspect in his case, all the way back to his childhood.

"I think the most important thing we learned in Ohio was that this former military guy is a survivalist. He's more likely to be hidden in some remote area than in this city."

"How do you know he's in Arizona?" I asked.

"Starting last year, there was a huge uptick on tips being called in. Some of them have proved to be very good tips. I can't say a whole lot about that, but it's why they've put us on the case here in Arizona."

"Does he have family in this area?" Greg wanted to know.

"We don't know of any family. He was in the foster care system as a child and never got adopted. We don't truly know who, or where, his biological parents are. A few people we interviewed mentioned a brother, but we haven't been able to determine who that is."

"So, they think he may have followed this brother to Arizona?" I surmised.

JJ just nodded slightly without giving any more details.

It was getting late so we moved to gather our belongings to leave.

"We'll walk you out to your car," JJ offered.

Once outside, Alexis walked me around to the

passenger side of the truck where I loaded Shadow into the backseat. JJ was talking to Greg from the driver's side. I could hear Greg lamenting over how hot it *still* was, even after midnight.

"Hey, hon…" Alexis said looking over the hood of the vehicle. She pointed to her next-door neighbor's home. "Was that car there earlier?"

"Yep, I noticed she has *company* tonight," he said mockingly in a sexy voice.

We all looked over and saw the large black Chrysler 300 sitting in Sasha's driveway. Of course, Greg had no idea what the relevance was since he didn't know the neighbors. Alexis and I wiggled our eyebrows knowingly, and giggled a bit. Then we hugged each other and said goodbye.

I climbed into the cab of the truck and we drove off.

"What was that about the neighbor?" Greg asked.

"Oh, Sasha. She's a client of ours and has been their neighbor for several years now. Really nice gal. Generally, she travels all the time, but of course more recently that has changed. She doesn't go out much these days, but Alexis has mentioned how many different types of vehicles come and go from her house. You know, *overnight visitors*," I teased.

He laughed. "You two are so nosey!"

"I know! It's actually Alexis. She thinks Sasha should be settling down by now."

"It's the both of you," Greg poked my arm, teasing me.

"Hey, maybe that's the screaming we heard? Maybe she was getting hot and heavy next door?" I said, giggling like a teenager.

"Do you really think it sounded like *hot and heavy* stuff?"

"Oh, I don't know! I'm just joking around…" I laughed

out loud, still feeling the effects of the margaritas and the fun time with friends. "So glad you stopped drinking hours ago. I know I couldn't drive right now."

We agreed it was a super fun night. Once we got home, we recreated our own version of what Sasha's *hot and heavy* activities might have been.

CHAPTER NINE

The next morning, we slept in a little longer than I normally would … but then again, I wouldn't have *normally* been up half the night.

"I was about to call the police," Bella stated, taunting me.

"What?" I looked at her very confused.

"Nothing. Just teasing you…" she laughed. Then she passed by, using her elbow to rib me, "I *hear* your visitor arrived yesterday."

I blushed from the tip of my toes. The heat and flushed rash-look quickly spread all the way through to my scalp. I said nothing, just moved to the coffee machine and poured myself a cup. Suddenly, I wished I didn't have a roommate, but the irony wasn't lost on me. Alexis and I were just joking around about Sasha's latest visitor, too. Karma!

By the time Greg walked into the kitchen, my roomie had already walked out the front door on her way to work.

"Coffee?" I asked, even though I knew that answer and already had a mug in hand ready to pour.

As I set his coffee mug on the breakfast bar, Greg thanked me and yawned, "Please tell me I'm not expected to do much today."

"I don't have anything on the agenda. The only thing I wanted to do was take Shadow for a walk later. But now, we have to wait until the sun goes down."

"Well, I just ordered some security cameras online and they'll deliver by end of day today."

"Wow, that was fast … when did you do that? And, more importantly, how much do I owe you?"

"I went to Amazon from my phone shortly after we talked about it yesterday. You're lucky to be near a distribution center—next day delivery. We only dream of that in the hills."

He got up and rounded the kitchen counter to where I was standing. He slowly reached around me from behind, pulled me close, and kissed the back of my ear. "We can work on some arrangement for paying me back."

I wiggled out, "No, no, mister! I'm paying you for those cameras. Don't try to seduce me into forgiving my debts!"

"Ok, ok," he said, hands up, stepping backward and laughing. "I'll make sure you get the receipt."

My phone started to ring.

"Hello, Mother," I answered, looking directly at Greg with my index finger in front of my lips. "Shhhssh," I mimicked.

"Libby, are you coming here today?"

"I wasn't planning on it. Are you okay?"

"Oh…" I could hear the strain in her voice and suddenly became more concerned. "Mom, what's wrong?"

"There's been another break-in. This time across the street."

"Is everyone okay?"

"Oh, yes. They weren't home at the time. But, Libby … this is getting close. I'm scared." That is not a common thing to hear from my mother. She's normally very self-assured and rarely shows fear.

"Ok, I'll be over within a half hour or so."

Against my better judgement, but because he stuck his bottom lip out and begged with cute puppy-dog eyes … Shadow, Greg, and I loaded up and headed over to Mom's house.

She was standing out on her porch when we pulled up. The look on her face was absolutely classic in Julia Madsen's playbook. Her hand moved up in front of her O shaped mouth, then she did a little clap, and I think she actually did a little dance. Then, she bounced off the front step and came right over to Trina's passenger-side door. We got our masks in place. Greg was barely out of the vehicle, and I kid you not, my mother leaped on him with a huge hug.

"Ohhh, I'm so happy to finally meet you!" she squealed.

I have to remind here that I've never spoken a word about him to her—*how does she know who he is?*

Greg looked at me slightly confused. I smiled back, shrugging my shoulders letting him know, *I had no idea.*

"My pleasure, Mrs. Madsen. It's an honor to meet you," he sweetly replied to her.

Jordan came out of the house and I realized immediately I had been set up. I had stupidly confided in Jordan at one point that I had met Greg and we were getting closer. She also knew he was due for a visit. *What was I thinking?*

Shadow jumped out of the truck and quickly ran to the front door, making herself right at home. We all followed her inside while my mother fawned all over Greg. This was so embarrassing; I wish I could have properly warned him. He was a trouper though; he was rolling right along with it all, and actually seemed to be loving the attention.

"Libby, why have you been keeping this delicious man a secret?" Mom cooed.

I guess this is the day for blushing. My cheeks were immediately hot once again.

"Maybe because of this?" I swooped my arm out in an arc that encompassed the scene.

"Oh, c'mon, Libby. Let me have a little fun."

Ugh. I really regretted answering my phone this morning. That's when it dawned on me that the whole phone call was fake.

"Was there even a break-in across the street?" I asked her.

"Oh, yes. Arthur and Mildred are quite shaken." She then looked to the floor, and then back up at me with a huge grin. "Well, ok … there was an incident, but maybe I wasn't as 'afraid' as I pretended to be on the phone. That was Jordan's idea … she knew it would work."

I punched my sister's arm.

"Ow!" she cringed.

"That's not fair. Please don't cry wolf again. I need to know when you truly need my help!" I wasn't really angry, I just wanted them to know I didn't appreciate the false pretense.

Jordan stepped up, "Don't blame Mom. And you're

right, we won't play around like that again." Then she gently bumped Mom's arm with her elbow. "Now that we've met Mr. Blue Eyes!" She busted out laughing.

They all laughed; Greg was taking everything in stride. I was the only one cringing at my family's behavior. We all moved into the kitchen and Mom poured water for me; everyone else wanted iced tea.

"So, Mom, what did the thieves take from the Schroeder's?"

"Silverware, some jewelry, and tools. Oh, and some gold spray paint from the garage also."

"Did you and Margie talk to the police? I know you started up the Neighborhood Watch officially now," Jordan asked.

"We think those backpack kids are part of this. Police didn't seem to care what we told them, though."

Greg was lost; we got him caught up on the backpack gangs casing the neighborhood. I then told them about my conversation the other day with the young woman I thought was a prostitute. I had meant to discuss this with JJ to see if he could help me identify Lanky and Big K, but he'd been so busy, and then I completely forgot.

"If you have a contact at the police department, maybe give them those names and I'll follow up," I suggested.

Mom perked up as though I just made her day. "I do! And, I will!"

My mother was getting a kick out of being part of the watch group. She proceeded to tell us all about the shenanigans that Margie and she had been up to. The other night, they sat out in Margie's enclosed front sun room and literally watched the neighborhood—hidden in plain sight, dressed in all black, and spying through night-vision binoculars.

"Mom, you need to be careful. It's one thing to stay alert and report things to the police, but please don't try to confront these people. Promise me," I pleaded.

"Oh, we won't do anything silly. I promise. Mostly, we're just having fun. What else do we have to do during this pandemic?"

I just laughed. She got me there, and I was having a great time picturing these two older ladies pretending they were some type of ninja warriors. I wanted to actually see this in action; maybe I'd come join them one night.

* * *

On the way home, Greg was still chuckling to himself. I'm certain the image of my mother must have entered his mind again. My phone rang through my car speakers and I used the buttons on my steering wheel to easily answer.

"Hi Alexis! You are never going to believe…"

She interrupted sounding extremely anxious. "Where are you, Libby?"

"Remember I have the day off…"

"No, where are you? Can you and Greg get to my house … immediately?"

I already had started the blinker to change lanes and catch the next turnaround. "Yes, of course. We are two minutes away. What's going on?"

"You'll see when you get here." She hung up.

Greg was visibly worried as we looked to each other, wondering what we were about to discover. I turned onto Lexi's street, and even though the house was toward the end of the block, I could see multiple emergency vehicles … EMT, ambulance, and police cars. We sped up and got closer, I saw it loud and clear—the crime scene investigation mobile unit. My heart raced. *What's happened? JJ … Joshua?* My mind quickly spun all different tales until I saw that they were at the house just next door to the Johnson's. *Sasha's home.*

Alexis was standing in her driveway and we parked next to her. There was a frenetic buzz of activity, but as busy as it was, the scene also appeared to be extremely well-organized. Crime scene tape encircled the entire perimeter of Sasha's home. As we got out from my car, I saw a gurney being wheeled to the ambulance. It was Sasha, being wheeled away—I could tell by the long black hair. That's all I could see; she was strapped down and there was no movement.

Shadow jumped out of the car and let out a bark toward the officers. I shushed her to not distract them from their important work.

"What happened? Have you been able to talk to anyone?" I asked Lexi quietly and gave my friend a quick hug. "Where's Joshua?"

"He's watching a video inside. Um, one officer came over when I walked outside. He wouldn't tell me anything. But, he asked if I heard any suspicious activity. I didn't hear anything; I had just got home not long before. They are coming back over here shortly for more questioning … want footage from our cameras." Her voice trailed off in disbelief.

"Where's JJ?" Greg asked.

"He was called in. There was another sighting of the Robinson guy."

It dawned on me right then that maybe we *had* witnessed something. "Lex, remember the scream last night when we were in the pool?"

Alexis' eyes got huge and she covered her mouth with her hands. "I completely forgot all about that!"

"We all need to tell them about our night. It could be relevant," Greg added.

"I can't believe I forgot … my mind is still fuzzy this morning. Not near enough sleep and one too many margaritas last night, I guess." My friend rubbed her temples as if to prove the headache she was experiencing.

"I thought you'd be at the spa this morning—didn't you have an appointment?" I asked her.

"I did. I came home just after because JJ was called in and we didn't have anyone to watch Joshua. It wasn't even five minutes after I got home that I heard all these vehicles pull up. Then I came outside to see … and called you." She was visibly distraught. Of course, she would be, this was a friend and client of hers who apparently had been harmed.

"Hey, it's really hot out here. Let's go inside and get some water and wait for the officers to come over." I took Alexis' arm and led her toward the house. Greg had Shadow's leash and we all went inside.

We didn't wait long. Officer Beth Lahey knocked at the door and I answered. Initially, she was a little confused, but as she began introductions for herself and her partner, Officer Sherry Talin, she suddenly remembered me and Alexis from the spa incident. I invited them in, introduced Greg, and of course, they remembered Shadow—who proceeded to get lots of love and attention.

"Unfortunately, we are investigating an assault on a neighbor of yours. Do you know Sasha Adams?" Officer Lahey asked Alexis.

"Yes, I do. We've been neighbors for several years. She is also a client of mine at the spa."

"When was the last time you saw Sasha?"

"Well, she had a massage session earlier this week. I'm not sure I've actually seen her since then. Although, I do see her occasionally leave in her car."

"Have you seen anyone else come to her home?" Officer Talin asked.

"Yesterday we noticed a large black sedan," Alexis looked to Greg. "What kind of car was that, Greg?"

"Chrysler 300," he stated.

I leaned forward. "Last night, Greg and I were here for a pool/movie night party with our friends. We went in the pool probably around eight-thirty?" I looked to Greg and Alexis for agreement. They both nodded. "It was just minutes into the movie when Shadow barked and we all thought we heard something. I think we would all agree it was a scream. However, when we paused the movie, we heard nothing."

"I ran inside to check on my son who was sleeping upstairs. Everything was quiet," Alexis explained.

Greg spoke up, "We convinced ourselves that it was sound from the movie we were watching—*Knives Out*—and that must have been what we heard. So, we got back in the pool, started the movie. Then, part way through, another shrill sound. Again, we collectively thought it was a scream."

"This time we all got out of the pool, dried off, and the guys—Greg, and Alexis' husband Officer Jeff Johnson, went out of the backyard through the side gate and walked up and down the block," I added.

Greg nodded his head and continued, "Everything was really quiet. We didn't hear anything, didn't see anything, the neighborhood was calm. None of us heard anything else the rest of the evening. Libby and I left here somewhere around midnight."

"Was the sedan you spoke of still in her driveway?" Lahey asked.

"Yes," we all answered in unison.

"Is there anything else you can think of that would help with our investigation?"

Alexis looked up from her tea cup. "I don't think I have anything to add, but can you tell us—is Sasha okay?"

"She will be okay. She is being treated for injuries; she's stable and should recover fine."

"What happened?" Alexis asked. "Was it the rapist?"

Both officers looked at each other and hesitated. Then, Officer Talin's eyes met both Alexis' and my own very pointedly. "Ladies, please be careful out there. We cannot confirm yet whether this crime scene involved the same rapist we are hunting for. We can't divulge more than that, but you need to be very careful."

Greg, Alexis, and I stared at one another. I think we were all in agreement that this hit way too close to home and yes, we were sufficiently nervous.

"One last question," Alexis asked, "what hospital was Sasha taken to?"

"She's at Desert Samaritan."

We walked the officers to the door. Shadow snuck out between their legs and ran to the edge of Alexis' property.

"Shadow!" I yelled. She turned to look at me, but then proceeded to sniff all the way along the driveway. "Shadow, get over here!" I followed her around the side of the house and under the crime scene tape that ran just between the two houses. Officers Lahey and Talin followed us too.

I whistled loudly and shouted, "SHADOW!" She was

nose to the ground, headed directly for Sasha's house.

Officer Lahey, walking just to the side of me, suggested we let her sniff around. "Remember, she found items at your business. Maybe she's on the trail of something? We don't know this isn't the same person … could be helpful."

Shadow wasn't running around out of control; she was just methodically smelling all her surroundings. Some of the crime scene investigators stopped and looked at her. Officer Talin held up her hand indicating it was okay and we continued to follow Shadow. Her super sniffer was actively leading her all along the perimeter of the house until she got to the side gate at the opposite side of Sasha's property. There, she jumped up against the gate and barked. Talin opened the gate and we all carefully walked through into Sasha's backyard.

There were two investigators back there as well and Officer Lahey stopped to explain why we were there. I followed Shadow to the far back wall. She jumped up to the wall and barked again. On the other side of the wall was an alleyway which ultimately led to another neighborhood street that ran perpendicular. Lahey spoke into her shoulder radio and asked for yet another officer to check out the alley.

Shadow stopped jumping and barking and went back to investigating the bushes that surrounded a spa closer to the covered patio and back door. The spa was uncovered as though recently used. We saw the investigators had several clear plastic bags sitting on the patio table that appeared to hold articles of clothing. They were marking each bag and sealing them. Shadow sat at their feet staring up at the guy holding an evidence bag.

"Shadow, don't pester … they have a job to do," I scolded.

Officer Talin asked the man to describe what he had just put in that bag and where he found it.

"Uh, this one? Pink bikini top. Found next to the spa," he replied as he held the bag up for all to see.

"What about those," she pointed to the table where three other bags sat.

"Black face mask in this one—found in that bush." He pointed to the bush that Shadow had just inspected. "A condom in that bag—found here on the patio. And, here we have a medallion of some sort. Looks like it has a cross on it. This was in the spa."

Shadow pawed the man's leg once, then turned and pranced away. *Did she just thank the man?* I'd never seen that behavior from my girl before. I excused myself and followed her back around the side of the house to the front yard, along the front of Sasha's garage, and then across to Alexis' side yard where she abruptly stopped.

She turned and got really excited, sniffing along the Johnson home, all the way to the back gate. She started digging at the base of a bush. I walked closer and that's when I realized there was black spray paint writing just under the window. Joshua's window. It was legible, but smeared and looked to me like, "NIG..." The last letter trailed off as though unfinished. Shadow was still fixated in the bush. I went over to her and saw there was also a water bottle in the bush. Just then, Officer Talin came around the corner.

"We'll need the investigators to bring another bag. Shadow found a water bottle in this bush," I pointed to the bush and then the wall. When I looked up to the officer, I found her staring at Alexis' house. "Oh, yes, and that— another tagging, it looks like."

"Disgusting," she said shaking her head.

Shadow took off around to the front of the house and went directly to Alexis' front door. I looked back to see that Talin was waving us on indicating it was okay; our work was done.

Greg and Alexis were waiting just inside the front door and heard Shadow when she jumped up against it, trying to push it open. By the time I caught up to her, she had made her way to the kitchen where we had put out water earlier. Lapping up a lot of water, she looked up at me with a satisfied smile on her face, and then plopped down right in the middle of the cool tiled kitchen floor. Apparently, her job was done.

"Where'd you guys go?" Greg asked.

I was shaking my head in bewilderment, "I think Shadow just tried to help solve a crime. I have no idea what she actually *did*, but the officers sure seemed pleased." I turned to Alexis, "I hate to even think this, but if I read the situation right, I think Officers Lahey and Talin believe that it could be the same guy who was at our business."

"Good girl, Shadow!" Greg had gone over and joined her on the kitchen floor, loving her up and scratching her belly.

"Lex … uh, I'm afraid there's something else." I hesitated. "Your house has been tagged. Black spray paint just under Joshua's window."

"What?" Greg said in surprise. "We went through that gate last night. We would have seen that!"

Alexis started shivering. She sat down. Her voice was shaky. "How does he know I live here?"

CHAPTER TEN

JJ got home just in time to see the mobile command center pulling out of their neighborhood. Greg was outside inspecting the painted wall when he heard him pull up in the driveway.

"What was that all about?" JJ asked, pointing to the exiting vehicles.

"Your next-door neighbor was assaulted."

"Oh my God, really?"

"Yes. Plus, this ..." Greg started walking and motioning for JJ to follow him.

"What the hell?" he blurted out when he saw the hateful writing on the wall.

"I know. Alexis is quite shaken. We all gave our account of last night, but they may still want to get your statement as well."

JJ nodded, gave another glance to the side of his house. "This was not here last night when we came through that gate!"

"I know, that's what I told the cops, too."

We headed into the house.

"Sweetie, are you okay?" He went straight over to Alexis and swept her into his embrace. She broke down crying, but once she settled a little, he continued, "Did they say *when* this happened?"

"You know, they didn't give us much. But, we did tell them everything we remembered from last night." She sniffled and grabbed another tissue.

"Guys, do you remember hearing Sasha and her guest in her hot tub?"

They all looked to one another. Almost in unison, they silently shook their heads 'no.'

"When Shadow and I were in her backyard, the spa had been used. I didn't hear anyone out there while we were outside."

JJ's head was shaking, "No, even when we thought we heard something, it wasn't that close. It sounded far off. Well, farther than right over the back wall. I mean these houses are all very close together … it's not *that far* from our pool to her hot tub, all things considered."

"Exactly," I agreed.

Greg came over to my side. "Should we leave these two alone to process this?"

I agreed and we got Shadow on her leash and said our goodbyes.

* * *

The last twenty-four hours had really drained me. Everything from the excitement of having Greg visit and a late-night party with our friends, which was all a great high; then the complete stress of the visit with my mother and ultimately learning that our friend was assaulted. I just didn't even know how to fully absorb any of it.

When we got home, Greg immediately started installing the cameras that had arrived. After that, we decided to spend the rest of the afternoon watching movies and relaxing. While Greg installed cameras, I had called Bella to update her and make sure Alexis' appointments were cancelled for the afternoon. It's a good thing I did because she did have another client showing up within the hour. Poor Alexis, all of this had really upset her. I let Bella know that if the client was upset with the rescheduling, or couldn't be reached and therefore showed up, I'd come in and handle it. Thank goodness I never heard back. I really didn't want to go anywhere.

We snuggled up on the couch and turned on Netflix. Before long, both of us were sacked out asleep. It must have been a couple hours because the next thing I knew, Bella came through the door and we were groggily greeting her.

"Sorry! Didn't mean to wake you guys. Wow, you look *tired.*" She smiled, put down her bags and went to the kitchen for some water.

"It's been quite a day," I said yawning. "I suppose I should start thinking about dinner though."

"Don't worry about me, I'm heading right back out. Meeting my study group and will probably be late." She fluffed up Shadow's fur, praising her, then skipped off to her bedroom.

"Are you hungry?" I asked Greg.

"A little. Honestly, I'd be fine ordering a pizza or something. You don't need to cook."

"Pizza sounds great! Can I make a suggestion though?"

He laughed, "Of course…"

"I'd like to take Shadow for a walk soon after the sun goes down when it isn't so hot." I checked my watch. "So, about an hour from now. We'll order online and schedule to pick up the pizza on the way back?"

"Sounds like a plan."

* * *

Greg was extremely confused as to why we drove to my mother's neighborhood to walk Shadow. He was even more perplexed when I asked him to wear dark clothes. Thankfully, he's the type of man who doesn't question me too hard, and he did exactly as he was asked to do.

"Couldn't we have walked in the desert behind your development?" he asked me as we were strolling along on Crescent Ave., one block north from where my mom lived on Capri Dr.

"Yes, we could have," I looked over to him and his question still lingered. "But, I wanted to see how active this drug ring is. Is she just paranoid? Or, is there a larger problem here?"

"Ah. And what about earlier when you mentioned 'Lanky' … or something like that?"

"Well, that's presumably the name of one of the bicycle-riding backpack guys."

I got the feeling Greg decided he didn't want to know any more … he stopped asking questions and just walked along my side.

Shadow barked. I jumped.

"What is it girl?"

She pointed to the house we'd just passed. It was a single story, white-painted brick 1960s ranch-style home. The entire front yard was rock that they had painted green. Did they really think it would look like grass? It didn't. I could see lights on in the house. Through the large picture window that faced the street, I could also see an elderly couple sitting on their sofa watching Wheel-of-Fortune. Shadow just stopped and stared at the house.

"Are you tired of walking already?" I asked her.

She barked again.

That's when I saw the elderly gentleman stand up and come to the window. He looked outside as I was trying to convince Shadow that we should go. The man pulled the drapes closed. Once we could no longer see inside the house, Shadow pulled to continue walking down the sidewalk.

"Maybe she just wanted to say hi to your mom's neighbors? Or she thought it was your mom's house? They all look alike," Greg wondered out loud.

"I suppose."

There wasn't any bike-riding going on tonight; we didn't see anyone out walking either. Of course, it was still pretty hot … maybe just not the night to be out. So, we walked back to the car. As I was loading Shadow into the backseat, Greg informed me of a note on my windshield. Ugh, neighborhood watch, most likely.

I unfolded the small sheet of paper, it read: STOP OR YOU'LL REGRET IT!

"Stop what?" I read it again. "What am I doing? Pretty

sure you can park along the street … there aren't any No Parking signs anywhere." I looked up and down the street.

"You're looking for young bike-riding individuals that shouldn't be in your mother's neighborhood," Greg repeated my earlier words back to me.

I was starting to believe now that I was on to something. This has to mean that Trixie, or whoever the tweaker was, had spoken to her buddies. That's the only way someone would know this vehicle, right? *Or, is this related to what's going on farther north in my own neighborhood?*

CHAPTER ELEVEN

"I cannot believe how fast this time went," I almost whined as we enjoyed a cup of coffee at the breakfast bar in my kitchen. Greg had just got back from my mom's where he installed her three security cameras.

"I know." He set down his mug and came over to stand in front of me. Taking my hands, he said, "It won't be much longer, and we'll be together again. Promise."

There's a huge part of me that always moves into this protective mode when I sense abandonment. Of course, I knew that Greg wasn't 'abandoning' me, but ever since my father died when I was sixteen, I struggle with goodbyes. The feelings bubbled up. The fear of never seeing someone you care for, ever again. It's powerful and I have to work at *not* pushing people away just because of my fear of loss.

"Yes, we'll be together very soon." I lowered my head so he wouldn't see my eyes welling up. "Can I make you breakfast?" I perked up and moved to get past him and over to the refrigerator.

"Your mom already fed me." He smiled. "Unfortunately, I'm going to have to take off. I've probably stalled as long as I can," he said apologetically.

My shoulders slumped and I closed the fridge doors. "Ok, we'll walk you out." Shadow immediately perked up from where she was lying—in the middle of the kitchen floor. She jumped up and wiggled her way over to him.

"Oh, yes … I'll miss you, too, sweet girl." He rubbed her head, reached into her nearby cookie jar and gave her a treat. "Take care of your mommy."

Once he was gone, I knew I needed to get back to work. No time to feel sorry for myself, missing my boyfriend. I need to keep my mind on work—both at the spa and also my own investigation of the crimes. I awoke this morning with a newfound resolve to take back control of my surroundings. Both Alexis and Sasha had been assaulted and terrorized; my home, our business, and the Johnson household had been vandalized; and my mother's neighborhood had seen theft and apparent drug related crimes. The police have their hands full, but for once, I think I agree with my mother—we citizens must take control of our neighborhoods and let the criminals know this isn't acceptable. *We will identify you, Mr./Ms. Criminal, and we'll assist the police in holding you accountable.*

First stop, the police station. As soon as I found the note on my car last night, I had handled it carefully and put it inside a plastic baggie as soon as we got home. I need to turn that over to Officer Lahey—it was clearly a threat.

She had a lot of questions. "This wasn't left at your house, but on your car in another neighborhood?"

"Yes, that's right."

"Any idea who would have written you this love letter?" she asked.

"I did talk to a young woman the other day. She was walking down the street—I'm calling her Trixie, but I'm not sure if that's her name or not. Prostitute? Could be a tweaker herself…"

"What did you talk to *Trixie* about?" Beth Lahey squinted her eyes and gave me a disapproving look.

"Well, I, er…" *What do I tell the police?* "Ok, um…"

"Spit it out, Libby. What shenanigans are you up to?"

"My mother is convinced there is a drug ring in her area. The police have been out there and my mom and her neighbor have started a Neighborhood Watch group." I took a sip from my water bottle before continuing. "I saw this girl one day as I was leaving the neighborhood. I may, or may not, have given her the impression that I was looking for someone to buy drugs from…" my voice squeaked a little and my sheepish grin made Officer Lahey break out into a wide smile.

"You? Do you really think that *you* could impersonate a real druggie? Look at you!" She was nearly doubled over laughing. When she caught her breath, she continued, "What did *Trixie* tell you?"

Feeling a little more confident because I *did* walk away from that conversation with names, I told her, "Well, I got a couple names from her and a vague area of town where at least one of them may live. There's a Lanky and also a Big K. I think Lanky is one of the drug runners … they actually bike around the neighborhood. Big K, I believe, is the dealer. She confirmed he lived over near Extension and Broadway." I pointed in the general direction—as though this police officer wouldn't know the layout of Mesa. I quickly lowered my arm, feeling silly.

Officer Lahey's laughter had ceased and she was staring wide-eyed at me now. "She actually told you about Big K?" I nodded. "We have a unit that has been trying to bust that drug operation for months now. And, you have a conversation with a tweaker and learn this information within, what, minutes?" I nodded again.

"I'm guessing that she mentioned that a lady in a silver 4Runner was asking about them. They took exception to this and left me this note." I held up the plastic baggie, wiggling it in the air.

All her laughter disappeared. I think I was relieved that she wasn't mocking me any longer, but the new and more serious tone had me equally nervous. "Libby. Please do not approach or interact with these people again. Promise me."

I nodded.

"Seriously. Tell your mother also. Even though they appear younger and ride bicycles somewhat innocently around the area, this drug cartel is nothing to mess around with. Big K and his guys are extremely dangerous. We have undercover officers working on this. Please don't get in their way. Now, I will give them this note, and we'll also analyze it as part of the investigation surrounding your business. Let us do our job and, I promise you, we'll let you know just as soon as we have information that we can share."

As though I had just been admonished by the school principal, I agreed and then made my retreat. *Now what? My plan was to snoop around and try to figure this out on my own.*

After leaving the station, I stopped by home and picked up Shadow and then we drove to work. I did have several appointments; this would give me time to devise my next course of action.

"Good morning, Bella!" I said as I walked in. Mr. Smith was waiting in the lobby for his wife to finish up with Alexis. "Good morning, Mr. Smith!" Shadow ran over to say hi to him as well. The Smiths are definitely dog people, and Shadow knows there's a good chance he will have a treat in his pocket. He greeted us both, and was already loving on Shadow as they played their 'cookie game.'

I laughed as she proceeded to con him out of the treats in his pocket and I continued straight through the door to our offices. Alexis had just come out of her massage room as I entered the office.

"Good morning, lovely," she said.

I walked to her and gave her a giant hug. "Good morning. How are you doing today?"

"I'm much better. It's been a tough couple of weeks, hasn't it?"

"That it has." I set my bags on the chair in the corner. "How's Sasha? Have you talked to her?"

"Still in the hospital. No, haven't talked to her … she's not taking calls, but the nurse confirmed she's stable and resting. I was going to call again this afternoon to see if it was possible to see her yet."

"I'm still shaken over all that. I also really want to know what exactly happened. Have they indicated what type of injuries she sustained?"

Alexis just sadly shook her head.

Later that day, after a full load of clients, Bella, Alexis, and I hung out in the relaxation room sipping tea. Shadow sat at our feet, seemingly exhausted as though she also had worked hard all day. I mean, I guess it must be hard greeting clients and receiving so much love. I suspected she also had consumed more treats than she should have.

"I've called the hospital; no visitors allowed," Alexis announced. "COVID protocol. I hadn't even considered that earlier. I really want to go visit Sasha."

"I know. That sucks!"

Bella was curious what we did know about Sasha's incident so we filled her in. We didn't know much, and were still waiting to learn when she'd be released.

Alexis took a sip of her tea, then said, "I'm going to offer for her to stay at our house. I can't even imagine going back to her place—if I were in her shoes."

"True. And, she may need help ... not knowing what her injuries are, who knows?" I added.

After an hour, we cleaned up and left work.

Several days later, Alexis got a call from Sasha asking if she'd be able to pick her up. I volunteered to go too.

My heart just hurt the second we drove up to the pick-up area near the front door. It also became quite apparent why she was in the hospital so long and why she hadn't taken calls. It took my breath away. She was physically in bad shape. Her head was completely covered in white gauze, and it wrapped all the way around and down below her chin as well. We could only see her purple and black, puffy eyes among all the bandages. Her arm was in a cast, which right now was also in a sling.

"Oh sweetheart!" Alexis was the first to speak as we got out of the car. I could see that she wanted to embrace her with a hug, but was hesitant because it appeared as though *everything* hurt.

Sasha immediately welled up with tears in her eyes. I felt the heat behind my own eyes, knowing the salty liquid brewing was imminent. Our poor friend.

"I'm a sight, aren't I?" she whispered with her mouth barely open, unable to move her jaw much at all.

"Well … you've probably seen better days. Most importantly, though, you *are* going to heal," I said quietly, with a slight squeeze on her shoulder.

With the assistance of a nurse, we loaded her into the car and buckled her in. As we pulled out, we were all silent. I definitely was taking in the gravity of the moment. I didn't expect to see her in this bad of shape.

"Did they catch him?" she asked quietly.

Alexis looked at me in the backseat from the rearview mirror and Sasha followed her gaze.

"We haven't heard anything," Alexis said. "Have the police gotten your statement?"

"Yes. Early on when I first arrived in the emergency room. Haven't seen them since."

I hesitated because I wasn't sure if she was ready, but eventually I asked what she remembered.

"Much of that night is foggy."

"Do you know the man?" I asked her.

"We met on Tinder," she whispered. "We'd had several dates—coffee dates—before the pandemic started."

"What is his name? Did you invite him over?" Alexis was curious.

She nodded her head and tears started falling again.

"Is this too much to talk about right now?" I asked.

She nodded her head again.

"Are you in pain, honey? Do we need to stop for any prescriptions, or...?" I asked.

"I've got everything I need. Yes, everything hurts. I've got a pretty bad head injury." Then, she pointed to her ribcage area, "Broken ribs."

"Oh, baby." Alexis visibly cringed when Sasha pointed out all her injuries.

We learned she had lacerations on her head, her brain swelled from the trauma and they had drilled to relieve pressure; her left arm and wrist were broken; she had several broken ribs, but thankfully none of them punctured her lungs. Her eye sockets had been fractured, her jaw was wired now, and there was severe bruising all over her body.

Slowly, she whispered, "I just can't forget his green eyes. That's all I see now." She winced at the pain.

Alexis startled—her eyes wide and her hand shook on the steering wheel as she looked back at me in the mirror.

"Do ... do you remember any tattoos?" I asked.

"I know there's something..." Wincing again, she took a breath. "I'm not remembering ... the police asked too." It was clearly difficult for her to speak. "Head foggy. Hard."

I remembered Alexis said her attacker had a cross tattoo, so that's why I asked. We could see how difficult it was so we changed the conversation and began asking about how we could help her. Were there family members she could stay with? We also both offered for her to stay at our own homes, if she preferred.

She closed her eyes, caught her breath, and slowly started again, "I appreciate you two," she squeezed Alexis' hand. "I'm not sure yet. It means the world to me that you are here now though. And I'm okay being at home—that's where I want to be."

It was obvious she was tired, along with the difficulty she had trying to talk, so we kept it short when we stopped at her house and got her settled in.

Alexis tried her hardest to get Sasha to reconsider but when all else failed, she stated, "I'm right next door. Please call if you change your mind—I'll come right over."

"Thank you so much ladies! I truly appreciate you." She gave us each a gentle hug and then we left her.

As soon as we got outside, Alexis turned to me, "Libby, I fear it's the same person who held me at gunpoint. The green eyes…" she trailed off.

"I picked up on your concern about that. I'm glad you didn't tell her about the tattoo—could influence her memory. I mean, a lot of men have green eyes … maybe it's not?"

"True. It's just the way she said it … they seemed to spook her as my attacker's green eyes terrified me."

"I just can't figure out *why*…" I said after several minutes of silence as we drove the car into Alexis' driveway.

"I know. I know…"

CHAPTER TWELVE

A few days later, it was finally the weekend again and I needed to spend some time at the spa doing laundry and cleaning up. Bella was off with her study group this weekend—they had some practical application tests they were studying for. I was amazed at the level of schoolwork there was to become an EMT. We all were very proud of how seriously she was taking her classes though.

Shadow loved going to work with me. As soon as we walked into the building, she immediately went on patrol, smelling every inch of the lobby area until she sat behind the counter with her nose pointed directly at her cookie jar.

"Ok, one cookie for now." I reached in and broke off a piece of the bone-shaped treat, made her wait for it, and then gently gave it to her using a closed hand and then slowly revealing the cookie. We were working on receiving treats gently and not snapping my fingers off. "Such a good girl, great patrol duty," I praised when she carefully took it from me.

I made sure the front door was locked and then we headed back to the office and massage room areas. We hadn't been there ten minutes when Shadow made her way back to the front lobby and began barking her head off.

"What … what are you…" I came through the frosted doors behind the front counter and saw a man standing at the door. *Michelle's husband?*

"Mr. Whitmore," I yelled through the glass, "we're not open today."

The expression on his face appeared as though he wanted to tell me something urgently. Even though I was initially hesitant, I decided to open the door. "Shadow, sit. Stay." She did as she was told; I unlocked and opened the door a crack. "Is everything okay with Michelle?" I mean why else would he be here?

"Can I come in?" he asked. Again, I hesitated.

"Sure, come in." I opened the door wider.

Shadow became restless and wanted to smell our guest. He didn't come across as a huge dog person—he hadn't even acknowledged her yet. "Shadow, sit. Stay." I said again when she started to get up.

His hands were in his pockets. He was looking at the ground. Gradually, he looked up at me. Then he made a move to pull his hands out and raise them. Shadow didn't like that at all. Despite her command, she instantly barked and stood up. Her ears pulled back and tail tucked.

"Mr. Whitmore, what can I do for you?" I was getting impatient.

His voice started out low, almost in a whisper. "It's all your fault."

"I'm sorry, what was that?" My head tilted sideways; my brow furrowed questioningly.

"She left me and it's all your fault!" he yelled louder.

Shadow growled, but stayed put.

"I- I don't know what you're talking about, Mr. Whitmore."

"*This place*. Ever since *this place*," he spat, "she's changed."

"I'm sorry, but I'm not responsible for anything going on in your marriage."

He started toward me. Shadow was having none of that. She jumped at him and stayed between the two of us, growling.

"You and that lesbian are running a sex business and now, you've converted my wife!!"

His green eyes looked like they were going to burst from the eye sockets. Shadow snarled, showing her teeth, growling; she pushed him toward the door.

"Get out now!" I told him. "I'm calling the police unless you leave this instant."

Shadow jumped up and nearly knocked him into the glass door; he turned, slammed open the door, and left.

Shaking, I quickly locked the door, then pulled my cell phone from my pocket and called Officer Lahey. I sat down at the computer on the front desk and pulled up Michelle's profile as I waited on hold. Once the officer answered, I explained everything that had happened and gave her the Whitmore address. Green eyes, 'lesbian', and sex business? It seemed this was exactly who had been targeting us all along.

* * *

Alexis was stunned. I stopped by their house after the police left. "*Why* would Michelle's husband do this?"

"Well, remember I told you that she quit her membership with us? I think this is exactly why. He's a nut job!"

I could tell Alexis was deep in thought and hadn't heard everything I said.

"The green eyes. Do you think he's the rapist? I mean, isn't that exactly how Sasha described her attacker, too?"

I thought for a few seconds. "I definitely think Mr. Whitmore is the one who spray painted our building. I think he could have been the one who threatened you. But, I am stopping short of thinking he's a rapist." I took a sip of tea, set down my cup and continued. "The way the man who held you at gunpoint hesitated, and then ran off scared, I just don't think it's the same person. I could be wrong, though."

Alexis pulled out her laptop and turned it on. After a few seconds, she asked again for the last name. She typed it in and continued searching different sites.

"What are you looking for?"

She was concentrating, then looked up. "The Arizona registered sexual offenders. If you've been convicted, you have to register and there are notifications about which neighborhoods they move into. Do you know his first name?"

"Uh, I believe she said Chase … no, Chester!"

"Ah, yep…Level 2. Convicted in Ohio. And, he has two violations of not registering on Arizona's list."

My jaw dropped. All of a sudden, I felt sick.

JJ walked in the room and saw our faces. "What's wrong?"

Alexis showed him the computer screen. "This is the husband of one of our clients. He confronted Libby this morning and we think he may be the one…"

JJ knew instantly what she meant. "I'll kill him!" he stomped, and then started pacing frantically.

"Shh. Joshua…" she quickly whispered, pointing to the living room where Joshua was playing.

"Did you call it in?" he asked, still pacing across the kitchen floor. I nodded my head.

"I don't want either of you alone at work, until this psycho is in custody, do you hear me?" His voice was stern, but quiet.

We both nodded our heads. JJ left the room. We stared at each other for a few moments before either of us spoke again.

"Who would have thought …" she finally spoke up.

"This is really crazy. Why on earth would he have a problem with *a spa*? We are *not* in a sex business. And what is up with the lesbian remarks?"

"I don't think we can make sense out of crazy, Libby. Some people just think differently."

"Well, I finished up what I had to get done there today, but were you going to head over there? If so, I'll go with you."

"Nah. I brought my computer home and I'll work on some accounting stuff from here. Did you have appointments today?"

"Nope, this weekend is free. But, we need to figure out how we're going to keep our clients safe and away from this craziness. Last thing we need is this wacko showing up when we do have clients in house."

"I'm just hoping that now that they have the Whitmore address, we won't have any more of these issues."

"Good point," I said, walking over to the kitchen sink. I washed out my tea cup and dried it. "I'm heading over to Mom's house now. We're going to have lunch and visit a little bit."

"Say hi to Julia!"

As I was pulling up to Mom's house, my phone rang.

"Hi Officer Lahey!" I answered.

"Libby. We spoke with Chester Whitmore. Do you have a moment?"

"Yes, of course." I waved my mom off, wiggling my phone, holding my finger up, trying to indicate that I was on the phone. She was waiting on the porch impatiently. "Go ahead."

Lahey proceeded to tell me all about her conversation with the Whitmores. Apparently, Michelle was still living in the house and she provided her husband with an alibi for each time we were targeted, except for the conversation this morning, which he wasn't trying to deny. He told the officers that he objects to this type of business being in his neighborhood and he wants it shut down.

"Of course, we told him that you have every right to operate your legal business where it is. We have warned him from contacting you, and since his wife is no longer a client, he has no right to be on your property at all."

I sat dumbfounded. Nothing was going to happen to this man.

"You can file a restraining order if you feel safer doing so …"

"People ignore restraining orders every day--what's the

point?" I was frustrated.

"You are correct that it's not one hundred percent effective. However, it does give us cause for arrest if he is found on your property again. Just think about it. I have a feeling he didn't like the visit he received this morning and he'll leave you alone now."

"I sure hope so."

I hung up, feeling the burden, but took a few deep breaths before I faced my mother.

CHAPTER THIRTEEN

The next morning, I was anxious so Shadow and I got up really early and went for a jog. It had been a few days so it was no wonder I was feeling anxiety creep in. I really wanted someone held accountable for the recent vandalism and especially the two assault cases that traumatized two of my friends. It was beginning to feel as though bad people were not being held accountable and I wanted to see that change.

We ran fast, winding through our neighborhood streets, and then out onto Power Rd., and through another development west of mine. On the way back, we approached Thomas Rd. and, looking across the shopping center parking lot, I could see our business at the far northeast corner. There was a man standing in front of the door—just standing there. We slowed down and I led Shadow toward the coffee shop at the corner; we slinked around the side of it where we could see Dharma Inspired Day Spa, but we couldn't be seen from that vantage point. I pulled my phone out and pressed Officer Lahey's number, which I had on speed dial by now. As it rang, I just prayed she'd be on duty early since she knew our case best. I didn't take my eye off the man standing in front of my business.

"Lahey." Sluggish and frog-throated, Officer Lahey didn't exactly seem as though she were sitting at her desk working.

"Officer Lahey? I didn't mean to wake you. Actually, I thought I was ringing your desk…"

"Libby?"

"Yes, it's Libby Madsen. Why did you answer if you're not at your desk?"

"Forwarded to my cell phone. What's wrong?"

"Shadow and I are out for our morning run. We are near my business … there's a man standing out front."

"What's he doing?"

"Just standing there. But, I think it's Chester Whitmore. I'm not approaching—we're at the coffee shop across the parking lot."

"If he's not breaking the law, why are you calling me?"

"Because I'm sure he's the one who has been terrorizing Alexis and me!"

"Libby, he had an alibi."

"Yeah, his *wife*. Are we confident in *that* alibi?"

"Libby, take a breath. Did you file the restraining order?"

"No. Not yet." I said defeated. *Why hadn't I done that yet?*

"Ok. Then there's nothing we can do. He has a right to

be in a public space." A big yawn and then she continued, "If you are in danger, call 9-1-1. If not, let me get a couple hours more sleep before my shift starts." She didn't sound happy as she hung up.

Shadow and I continued our jog and headed out away from the businesses to get back to the neighborhood. I couldn't help but think that Chester *had* to be the one doing all this. The way he spoke to me. He definitely had a grudge against us. I just wished we could pin the vandalism on him. And, was he capable of attacking Alexis, or Sasha? I don't know, but he is definitely guilty of something and, right now, that something is standing in front of my business and giving me creepy goose-bumps all over. I'll head to the police station later today and file for a restraining order to keep him off the property at least.

By the time we made it home, my mom was calling.

She quickly told me someone was outside her bedroom window very early this morning. There was a scratching noise and she swore she saw a shadow. I asked if she was okay and she said yes. "I know what I heard, Libby."

"Ok, let me shower, I just got back from my run. I'll be over in about forty-five minutes. Keep the doors locked. Don't answer the door for anyone you don't know."

As I pulled into her driveway, I noticed an old man sitting out on the porch next door—must be Mr. Knight. It hit me then that no one had called me back after I left the note on his door more than a week ago. So much had happened, I completely forgot. Well, no better time than the present—I put on my face mask, got Shadow out of the car, and then proceeded next door.

"Hello!" I said as we approached. I just got a blank stare, no response at all. "Hi, my name is Libby," I shouted a little louder in case he hadn't heard me the first time. I stopped just off the patio, staying well-distanced since I could see he didn't have a mask on.

"Good morning." His voice was flat. He appeared tired and didn't have the ability to hold himself upright very well. Shadow whined and held her head down. She was oddly subdued for meeting a new person. I petted her with a *good girl* and held tight to her leash anyway.

"My mom lives next door and I'm visiting. I wonder if I could just ask you a few questions?"

Before he could speak, the door opened and a very tall, thin man—probably in his forties—came barreling through the front door, but before he made it all the way out to the patio, I had heard him saying, "Dad, what are you doing out here in the heat? Let's come back inside and get your breakfast." The door slammed and he was looking right at me, confused. "Oh, I didn't realize Dad had company." Shadow jerked forward and barked. The fur all along her spine stood on end.

"Shadow, sit." I nodded to the stranger, "Hi, I'm Libby Madsen. This is Shadow," I looked down at the uneasy canine. "My mom lives next door." I pointed in the direction of her home and waited for some recognition. Since I left my name and number on the note last week, I expected that might trigger the memory that they never did call me. It didn't.

"What can I do for you?" The thin man didn't offer his name and he was clearly skeptical of me. Shadow lurched forward again, teeth bared. I gave a short yank to the leash and told her to sit.

"Well, this is going to sound very strange. I, um…" I hesitated trying to remember what last week's issue was. "My mom was saying that you are, um … building a gate. She thought she heard that you were putting this in through her wall? To use her pool…" As I said it, I couldn't help but hear how crazy that sounded.

Tall guy started laughing. "Well, that's crazy. No one here said that. And, I can assure you that we aren't going to access her backyard. Or pool."

"Ok, thank you! I needed to hear that directly from you because it just sounded so 'out there.' Honestly, I just don't think the isolation from the pandemic has really done any of our parents much good." I nodded my head toward his father and my mom's house. "She really needs more to do."

He chuckled again. "Yes, that is probably true." He reached out to help his dad up. The elderly man looked confused, and then struggled to stand. Once he was steady, his son indicated to go on inside. "That's why I moved in here with dad. There were already a variety of health issues, but since the pandemic started, his dementia has gotten so much worse. I guess in his 90s, what else can you expect? Most days, he doesn't even know who I am—did you see that look he gave me when I held out my hand to help him up?" I nodded. "Yep, we have some rows over why I'm in his house. He just doesn't remember who I am most days. Is your mother headed down that path?"

"Oh, no … she's still doing very well. 70s. Before this virus started, she was traveling, playing cards with friends, and was extremely social."

"Oh, she still gets out! She and that one over there." He pointed to Margie's house. "They love being the neighborhood spies these days. I haven't joined those outdoor Neighborhood Watch gatherings yet. Too much to do just keeping an eye on Dad."

I didn't know what to say about the busy-body comment so I just thanked him for his time and wished them well. Walking away, I felt a sadness. What would it be like to not have your parent recognize you? That's a horrible ordeal for families dealing with dementia or Alzheimer's.

"Well, I wondered where you went! I looked outside and saw your car, but couldn't see you. I didn't want to open the door." Mom was wringing her hands and had a frown on her face until she realized Shadow was seeking her attention. She bent over and started petting her. "Oh, what a good girl! It's always so nice to see you!"

"We just had a nice little chat with your neighbor," I explained.

"Was it him at my window this morning?"

I hadn't even thought of that, but I'm sure it wasn't. "Nope, I just wanted to understand their plans for that gate you told me about." She stood there staring at me with a blank look.

"What gate?"

Oh boy. My thoughts went straight to the conversation I'd just had with the neighbor.

"Ok. Why don't you tell me what happened this morning? Walk me through it." Anything to change the subject. She proceeded to take me into her room, showed me the window, and imitated the scratching sound by moving her nails along the wall.

"And, you said you saw a shadow? Can you describe it?"

"I thought it was a person."

"What made you believe that? Was the shadow in the

shape of a person's head, body, or…?"

She got irritated. "I don't know, Libby. I just *know* there was a person outside!"

"Ok. Why don't you go get us some iced tea in the kitchen? I'm going to go outside and look around near your window." She agreed and we both went about completing our tasks.

I began to question myself—is her agitation new? Has she always gotten this worked up? Why were Mr. Knight's son's comments now making me think my mom has dementia?

Shadow and I walked through her backyard over to her bedroom window. There was an overgrown shrub just to the right side of her window and I noticed that it rubbed up against the house. Was there wind last night? I couldn't remember. Shadow immediately ran in and around the bush, sniffer in overdrive. I searched for any evidence of footprints or any sign that someone might have been on the side of her home. The ground was covered in tiny pebble rock that had partially washed away so there were bare spots of dirt. I didn't see anything that suggested a shadowy figure had been there, and Shadow also didn't seem to be concerned, so we walked back inside.

Mom handed me my iced tea and I took a sip. "It sure is getting hot out already," I commented, while brushing off sweat from my brow with the back of my other hand.

"Well, what did you see? Was someone there?"

"Mom, I'm sure you heard something," I started gently. "The shrub over there could be trimmed back so it's not scratching against the house. I'm sure that's all it was."

She didn't look convinced, but pondered what I'd said for a second. "What about the shadow I saw. That bush isn't as tall as my window."

Good point. "I'm not sure about that. But, why don't we take one of the cameras Greg installed and we'll point it down that side of the house?" I suggested.

"I don't even know how those things work! So frustrating."

"That's okay. I can help, if you'd like."

Greg had bought her three new cameras the last time he was here. I'm not the expert at these things, but I'm sure it doesn't take a rocket scientist to move one of them. We walked around and decided that there was a camera already in the backyard near the side yard. Perhaps I could position it in a way that would work. I set out to complete the job while my mom followed me around and talked nonstop.

"Margie is sure one of the bikers is living here in the neighborhood. She said she's seen him every morning early and he's always coming from that direction." She pointed east of her house and then pivoted to point to the west. "And, he rides right on past her house. She sees him out of her front window."

Struggling with holding the camera, screwdriver, and picking up the screw I'd dropped twice now, I climbed back up the ladder and asked, "What does he look like?"

"She said he always wears black. One of those sweatshirts with a hood so she never quite saw his face or anything. We both think that's stupid in this heat—who wears black, heavy clothing in the middle of the summer in Arizona?" She tsked, took a sip of her tea, and continued with a chuckle. "She also said it looked like he stole a child's bike. He barely fits on the thing."

I had already observed that it appeared as though overgrown children were riding around the neighborhood.

Guess I just thought it was a trend. Larger guys with smaller bikes. Why had I not considered that they were actually stealing them from children? But, wait … there aren't children in this neighborhood. Didn't matter, she had already moved on to her favorite subject.

"So, how's Mr. Gorgeous?" she teased.

"Busy right now—those fires up north are keeping all the forest service personnel working very hard."

"When is he coming back?

"I'm not sure. Completely depends when they allow him a day off."

"When are you getting married?"

"Mom! We just started dating! Three months is not nearly enough time to make a decision like that." Although, even despite my fierce independence and fear of commitment, I found myself constantly missing him and wishing he were around more.

"Just don't push him away … he's a keeper, you know?" she winked and turned to go inside. "If you had done what Jordan…"

Ugh. I tuned her out while I tightened the last screw and climbed down the ladder. Exactly what I didn't want— Mom in my personal business. Does one ever get old enough where this intrusion stops bothering?

I went back inside to fire up the app on my phone. After several more tweaks to get the exact position, I gathered the tools and ladder, put them away in the small shed, and headed back inside.

"Ok, I will monitor your cameras—we'll figure out what you heard." I gave her a kiss to the forehead, asked if there was anything else I could do for her, reminded her to keep her doors locked at all times, and headed out the front door.

As I was backing out of the driveway, Shadow barked. I caught movement over at the neighbor's house. *Was that Trixie the tweaker who just walked inside?*

CHAPTER FOURTEEN

Back at the spa, I ran into JJ on the way in. Shadow pulled me up to the front door, eager to see her friend.

"Well, hello there, Libby … Shadow!" His smile was a welcome sight and made me miss Greg even more. The two of them had quickly become friends—and now, I thought of the four of us as a friends unit and wished we were all together.

"Good morning!" I checked my watch, *was it still morning?* "Er, I mean afternoon. Wow, where is the day going?"

"I know what you mean. Had a stakeout overnight near the city center, last known sighting of our perpetrator, so I've slept the morning away." He held the door open and we walked in, greeting Bella on our way through to the office area. Shadow stayed behind with her—probably since she's closest to the cookie jar.

"Libby, this case keeps getting stranger. This guy is on the run for fifteen years; his past is checkered with theft, assault, then murder. It's possible he's being hidden by a well-known drug cartel. Possibly even involved in prostitution from what I saw overnight." His eyes were wide with surprise.

"You'd think that if you're on the FBIs Most Wanted list, you would choose a lifestyle, or profession, that *doesn't* bring attention to you," I stated.

"Exactly. Where has he been all these years and *why* has he now shown up in Arizona? It's been a fascinating case to say the least. Anyway, I'm here to pick up my beautiful wife for lunch. We're heading to the park to enjoy some nice fresh air. Wanna join?"

"Oh, that's so sweet. But, no…I got a late start. Been at Mom's all morning rearranging cameras and listening to her tales of someone lurking outside her window."

"Oh no! She needs to be careful."

"Yes, I know. She is taking this Neighborhood Watch group so seriously, I think it's also getting her a little more paranoid than she'd normally be. I don't want to say that though—because she does need to be careful. Anyway, I'm going to monitor her cameras and we'll see if there's anything to all this."

"Hey there gorgeous!" Alexis said in her quiet voice, as she walked out of her therapy room and straight into the arms of her husband. "Let me finish with my guest," she pointed to the door she had just closed, "and then I'll grab my purse and we'll go."

JJ and I said our goodbyes and he headed to the front

lobby. I went about settling in and getting ready for my next client.

The afternoon sped along. I came out of my therapy room from my final appointment and saw that Alexis and Sasha were lounging in the Serenity room with a cup of tea. I walked across the room to give Sasha a huge hug.

"You are looking very well!" I exclaimed, noticing that the pink had returned to her cheeks. She didn't look near as gaunt and the bandage was finally removed from her head.

"Anyone would after one of her gentle, relaxation treatments," she bent her head toward Alexis, acknowledging her friend and therapist. "She is a life saver!"

"Yes, that I know," I agreed and grabbed a cup of tea. I saw my client over to the changing room. Bella would check her out at the front desk.

When I rejoined them, Sasha was quietly telling Alexis more about that night.

"I just never thought I'd find myself in a situation like that. I'm generally a decent judge of character. I completely missed the mark this time." She hung her head. "I mean, this guy on one of our first dates shows up in a truck with probably ten bikes in the back. When I asked why he has so many bikes, he explained he's donating them to the local Boys and Girls Club just after our lunch together. My heart swooned—he was sweet, philanthropic, and super handsome. I never saw it coming."

I reached over and rubbed her back. "Hey, this is not your fault. You know that, right?" She looked up and slightly nodded before her gaze moved down again. "To rough you up like he did, the man is a psychopath. There's *nothing* you could have done to change that."

Alexis agreed, and took Sasha's hand. "Sweetie, I know you said you regret using an online dating app, but honestly, it's not even that." She took a deep breath. "Unfortunately, you could have met this psycho anywhere. Just as you said—he was very charming on the several dates you had in public."

"It'll take a while for me to process. I hear what you both are saying, and I do appreciate your support. Right now, I can't help but kick myself. I feel so stupid." She welled up with tears.

"That's understandable," Alexis gently stroked the back of her hand. "Have you reached out to the therapist yet?"

Sasha spoke through her tears. "Not yet."

Shadow and Bella walked into the room. Sensing she was sad, Shadow zeroed right in and gave her attention to Sasha. She nudged under her elbow coaxing the human to pet her. A huge smile broke out across Sasha's face and she quietly continued to stroke the dog. Bella said hi on her way through to clock out and pick up her stuff from the office.

Alexis perked up, "You know, I've been attending group therapy. Would you like to join me? It might be a start…" Sasha nodded in agreement. "Ok, next session is tomorrow night. You can ride with me."

"Ok, I'd like that."

"I attend that group too," Bella said over her shoulder as she passed by them. "I'll see you guys there!" She headed off for school.

"Shadow and I need to get home," I stood, went to the office for my purse, and then tried to pry Shadow away from Sasha. My sweet girl was the antidote for sadness, that's for sure. "Are you two heading out soon?"

Alexis nodded her head and then looked to Sasha, "Yes. Let's all walk out together?" Sasha agreed and I waited a minute for Alexis to gather her belongings. We shut everything down and walked to the front door.

Just outside on the sidewalk in front of our place, Bella stood talking to Chester. When we opened the front door, we heard her getting a tongue lashing. Shadow growled.

"Hey, hey! Get out of here … you are NOT welcome at our business!" I yelled, boldly approaching Chester, allowing Shadow to lead the way. "I've already called the cops. GO!" It took all of my strength to hold Shadow back. She was baring teeth and snarling at Chester.

"No need to call the cops," he spat back. "Get away, dog!" He kicked at the dog, but missed.

I was going to lose my shit. "Get. Out. Of. Here. NOW!!!" I screamed. Shadow frantically barked and lunged. I held tight.

The hate that emanated off the man flared from his bright green eyes. I stood my ground though and eventually he broke my gaze and moved to leave.

"Good girl, Shadow. He's a *bad* man." I petted her head. She was still growling and her eyes followed him to his car. She didn't stop growling until his car peeled out of the parking lot and was out of sight.

I turned around to my friends. Alexis and Sasha stood there frozen in place, trembling. Bella was pissed.

"Alexis. Oh, my goodness, you are shaking. Here, let's go back inside. Bella, here, help me." She took Shadow's leash and I had Alexis lean on me as I assisted her back inside. Once we were in, I locked the door and we proceeded through the building, back to the sofas. "Bella, call Officer Lahey." I handed her my phone.

"Hey, hey … it's okay. He's just a bully—and he's gone now." I tried to soothe her, but she was violently shaking now and her brown skin was ashen all of a sudden. I wrapped a shawl around her shoulders and took her in my embrace and just held her tight. I reached out my hand to Sasha, "Are you okay?"

"Shaken, yes. I'm okay though." She sighed. "Who was that guy?"

"Police are on their way," Bella said coming back in the room. "Alexis, here's some water…"

I let go of my friend. She was in shock, but she slowly took the water and lifted the glass to her mouth. After several seconds, she took a deep breath.

"He … he," she caught her breath again. "Tha… that's, th … the man." A little cry squeaked out. "His … eyes," she pointed to her eyes. "I know it's him, Libby." Then, she looked down at Shadow. "Shadow … knows … too." She grinned at our sweet girl who had squeezed in by her legs and was laying down on her feet.

Bella heard the knock at the front door. Soon after, Officer Lahey and Office Talin both followed her to where we were sitting.

"Tell us what happened," Talin directed her question toward me, but then stared at Sasha as though she was trying to remember where she knew her from.

We relayed the whole scenario and Alexis identified Chester as her attacker from a few weeks ago. Although she had stopped shaking, the officers could see she was still terrified.

"Okay, we need you three to come down to the station for an official statement," then Office Lahey looked pointedly at me, "and we're going to file that restraining order *tonight*." I hung my head knowing that I hadn't helped the situation by delaying the task that could help get this man arrested.

We followed the officers out. I took Shadow home and then joined the others at the police station.

CHAPTER FIFTEEN

Between the pandemic, missing persons, vandalism, Mom, and my friend's trauma…I'm ready for this year to be over!" I exclaimed to Greg on the phone the next morning.

He sighed. "I can't imagine how you are managing all this."

"If it's not one thing, it is very literally another. Anyway, that's why today I'm just hiding at home with Shadow and I don't want to go out into the world. It's too 'peopley'," I chuckled at my own humor.

"Peopley? That's a new one—I like it! Well, I've got to agree … and we need a break at some point. So much drama going on, isn't there?"

"How are the fires?" I asked. I hadn't kept up with the

local news at all.

"We're down to one—thank goodness, the monsoons have started and are pumping moisture up here in the hills."

"Yeah, you get rain. We get the dust storms."

"It should slow down for me soon. We really need to get together once we're able."

"Absolutely agree." I sighed, wishing it was sooner than later. I went on to tell him about mom's 'shadow' at her window and moving the camera. We chatted for a few more minutes and then it was time for him to get to work.

My entire plan was to watch Netflix in my jammies all day and ignore the world outside my door. That lasted about five minutes.

"Hi, Mom," I answered my phone.

"Libby, where are you?"

"I'm at home."

"Oh good, can you check my cameras? Is there footage of someone in my pool during the night?"

"What? Someone was in your pool?"

"Well, that's what I want you to find out. I *know* I heard some splashing around … sometime in the middle of the night, but I didn't want them to see me so I stayed hidden in bed."

I breathed really deep before I said another word. *Why wouldn't she call the cops if someone was in her backyard? Ugh!*

"Mom, are you sure it wasn't a dream?"

"Libby! No!"

"Ok, ok. Then why wouldn't you call the police?"

There was a long pause.

"Mom?"

"You don't believe me, do you?"

"It's not that, Mom. I'm worried that if you are hiding in fear—why wouldn't you call for help?"

"Well, I'm calling now. Can you help me?"

My patience was waning, but of course I was concerned. "I'll check the cameras … and I'm on my way over. I'll bring lunch—it'll probably be about an hour by the time I shower and leave." I hung up wondering if she ever calls my sister, Jordan, about these types of issues. Doesn't matter. I jumped in the shower and got ready to head over there. I decided Shadow could stay home for a couple hours on her own.

When I turned off Power Rd., then onto the main street outside my mom's development, I saw the neighbor's son walking down the road with a woman. As I passed them, the raven-haired woman blew a gigantic blue bubble. *Trixie!*

I slowed down and turned a street earlier than I wanted just to get positioned where I could see them. I pulled into a business parking lot across the six-lane divided road and parked in a space facing them. They slowed their pace and hung around the bus stop. Two others—a woman with a young son—were standing there as well. No bus in sight as far as I could see.

I slumped down in my seat slightly and observed them talking. It appeared to be getting a little animated, but of course, I couldn't hear from where I was. Just then, a black Chrysler pulled up to the bus stop and they got in. I wasn't prepared for that, but proceeded to quickly start up Trina and move out of this parking lot onto Power Rd., where they had turned south.

I rushed to get through the light at the intersection and then followed them down to Southern Rd. staying a few cars behind. They turned right onto Southern and so did I. Now, I was right behind them, so I slowed down a bit trying not to be noticed. Of course, they both had seen my car before—Trixie, and ... *what was his name ... he never told me. Well, she hadn't told me her name either; I named her. So, I'll call him Tall Boy. Actually, maybe that wasn't the best of names because by the looks of it, the driver of the Chrysler was also quite tall.*

From behind, I could see the heads of both beanstalks—it appeared to me that their heads nearly hit the car's roof—one in the driver's seat and the other in the passenger seat. I couldn't see Trixie's head, but I had seen her get into the backseat. We drove along for quite a while and I managed to keep sight of them despite all the intersections we passed through. We were now driving into the heart of Mesa.

The traffic picked up and I changed lanes several times, dodging slower cars so I could keep up. They approached Extension Rd., and turned right. The light changed so I stopped, looked for traffic, then turned right on the red since it was clear. I could see that, several blocks ahead, the black car took another right. I made the same turn and then saw them about quarter of a mile ahead turning left. I followed. When I got to Vineyard and followed the curve in the street to the left, I didn't see the Chrysler anywhere.

I drove slowly looking at each driveway, trying to see down each street that intersected with this one. There were several and they could have turned on any one of them. Dangit! I went to the end of Vineyard, turned around, and then came back, turning on the first street ... driving slowly, making my way through the entire neighborhood. It was an older community—the small houses were a bit run down and most had multiple vehicles scattered about the properties as well as lining the streets. I never saw a newer black vehicle like the one I had followed.

My phone rang and that was the first time I realized that it had been more than an hour since I spoke to my mother.

"Hi, Mom, I'm on my way ... stopping to get us some sandwiches at Schlotskys, okay?"

"Oh, that sounds good. I was worried."

"Be there soon. No worries."

I hung up, and then verbally instructed my navigation system to find the closest Schlotskys—I better giddy-up!

When I pulled up to her house, I could see the old man next door on his front porch. Mom was peering through her blinds at her front window. She saw it was me and came outside.

"I was getting worried, Libby."

"Mom, I just talked to you ... told you I was on the way," I reminded her as we walked back inside the house. I gave a wave to the elderly gentleman next door but wasn't sure if I actually got a wave in return. No matter.

She looked a little bit confused and said, "Oh, that's right."

Ignoring the confusion, I started unloading the bag of sandwiches and chips. She poured some iced tea and we sat down to eat. She told me all about the splashing of water during the night, saying that she could hear it from her room. I asked if there was evidence this morning of water outside the pool ... or anything suspicious. There wasn't. I couldn't imagine from her room at the opposite end of the house to where the pool is in the backyard that she would be able to hear anything—*if people were out there.* More importantly, I couldn't imagine that anyone would come into her backyard specifically to swim, this just didn't seem plausible.

"It's probably that guy next door."

"The old man?" I asked incredulously. "Mom, he can barely move … I can't imagine him climbing over a wall. Your gate is locked."

"No! The younger one. I know he told you he was Mr. Knight's son, but I don't believe that. In all these years— he would have mentioned a son to me, or one of the neighbors, at least. Nope, no one has heard of this *son* … everyone is talking about it."

Well, this was news to me. I imagine that she had spoken to her watch group and got them riled up too, most likely. I finished my sandwich, but Mom was still slowly working on hers. Knowing that the younger man was not at the house next door at the moment, I excused myself and told Mom I'd be right back; I'd try to find out more from Mr. Knight.

George was still on his porch swing when I came outside. I waved again. Still nothing.

"Hello!" I tried projecting loudly. His head turned toward me as I approached his walkway. Again, I stood at the base of the porch steps and away from direct contact with him. "Hi, I'm Libby—remember me from the other day?"

He nodded and kept swinging.

"Where's your son today?"

He looked at me, confused, then stopped swinging. "I don't have a son."

"Oh. Who was the gentleman I met the other day?"

"I have no idea." He started to gently swing again.

"He's taking care of you, right?"

"I guess. He says he is," he grumbled.

"Mr. Knight—are you okay? Do you feel safe?"

He stopped swinging and just stared at me for several uncomfortable moments. His face was splotchy and red and I could see he was sweating.

"I'm not sure I understand your question."

"If this person isn't your son, did you invite him to stay with you? Is he being nice to you?"

"Oh, that. Yes, he's nice enough. Brings me food so I don't have to cook. I don't get around like I used to."

"What does he do for a living?" I decided to try a different line of questioning hoping he would open up to me more now.

"No idea."

"Where is now?"

"No idea."

Well, that was fruitful. I hesitated for a moment. Something wasn't right, but I couldn't put my finger on it. The man seemed physically okay. His 'son' said he had severe dementia so I wasn't sure what to believe—they very well could be related. I tried a different tactic.

"It's sure hot out here, Mr. Knight. Can I help you inside the house?"

"Sure."

I grabbed my mask from my jeans pocket and put it on, then I walked up the two steps and over to the porch swing. I braced myself and helped him up. He wasn't a light individual, but I was strong enough to get him up and once he was steady, he used his nearby cane to assist. I held onto his other arm *just in case*.

When we made it inside the living room, it was evident that the place had not been cleaned in an awfully long time. Other than that, it wasn't very cluttered; it appeared that Mr. Knight lived quite minimally. There was an ancient sofa along one wall and what appeared to be a newer recliner just south of the couch. That was clearly his chair and he was already beelining toward it.

"Can I get you some water?" I asked.

"That would be nice."

"Ok. This way?" I pointed through the doorway off to my right, and started walking that direction when he nodded. "When is your son due back?" I shouted from the kitchen as I took the opportunity to snoop around unchaperoned.

"He's not my son."

"Ok, when is your caregiver due back?" I rolled my eyes. *Sheesh!*

"He usually leaves for several hours. Can you put ice in that water?" he shouted.

"Certainly."

I saw a stack of papers on the kitchen table and decided I needed to snoop, er, straighten up … electricity bill, some coupon flyers, an AARP communication, and a banking statement—all in George Knight's name. From the items in the kitchen, I didn't see any evidence of this other person who was living with him. I was hoping to find a name.

"What's your roommate's name?" I shouted so he could hear me.

"No idea."

Another eye roll. The dementia story must be true

because who just accepts someone staying with them and not knowing the first thing about them. Likewise, who stays if they *aren't* family. He seemed difficult to deal with. I delivered the ice water to the man and asked if I could use his restroom. He pointed down the hallway.

The house was fairly small; it was a short hallway … two bedroom doors and the bathroom. Since he couldn't see me once I turned down the hallway, I 'got lost' and started snooping more. George's bedroom was simple—a twin size bed, a small dresser, and a nightstand. That was it. Nothing on the nightstand or dresser top. Bed was perfectly made. The next room was a disaster—bed unkempt, clothes all over the floor, and that dresser top was cluttered.

I visually inspected the mess—bubble gum wrappers, matches, cigarettes, receipts, and food wrappers. I did find a water bill that had the name Leon Knight on it. Hm, maybe he's the son after all? Same last name anyway.

After making a play of flushing the disgusting toilet, and then actually scrubbing my hands, I joined Mr. Knight back in the living room.

"George, does Leon like to swim?"

"Who's Leon?" he asked.

"Your friend that lives here?"

"I don't have friends. And no, they don't swim." He was getting grumpier by the second. I'd probably overstayed my welcome so I asked if he needed anything else. When he grumped no, I left.

I walked back into my mom's house.

With hands on hips, and a frown on her face, she said, "Where did you go?"

"Remember, I went to talk to the neighbors. Wanted to

see if they used your pool. They didn't."

"And, you think they are just going to tell you? They're sneaking around. A girl and a guy. Maybe not even from that house next door, I don't know." She sat on the sofa and had that pouty look that told me she was not happy with me.

"Ok. Mom, I don't know what to do here. You wanted me to come over…" It hit me; I never checked the cameras! "Hold on, let me check this really quick."

I opened the app on my phone and looked up the backyard camera. There were no 'events' to indicate saved footage of motion or sound. I scrolled through the timeline beginning around nine o'clock last night when it was mostly dark. Slowly, I scrolled through hour by hour until the sun came up this morning. Nothing. Just to be sure, I went back over everything one more time, even more slowly. *Wait, what was that?* There was a shadow that came from the east side of her patio briefly, then disappeared. It wasn't large so I ruled out a human being. The moonlight was quite bright in the footage, but the change in lighting appeared to be higher than the camera which would indicate something on the patio cover or maybe even flying. It had to be an owl or some nocturnal predator.

"Mom, I don't see anything that indicates someone was in your pool. You probably were dreaming and it seemed realistic."

She stared at me blankly for a few seconds. Then, quietly, "Libby, I know what I heard."

"Ok. I believe you." I reached out and took her hand. What else could I say? I didn't want to upset her, but so far, I could not prove that anyone was physically in her backyard. "Oh, hey … I forgot to mention, but JJ will come by and trim that bush by your bedroom window."

"He's so sweet." She moved her hand away from mine and moved to get up.

"Mom, do you need anything else while I'm here? I've got to get to work soon."

"No, you've done enough."

With that, I ensured her back door was still locked, gave her a kiss on the top of her head, and locked her front door before I closed it. I couldn't shake the feeling that there was more going on next door. But, in the end, none of it was really my business. My mom was fine, even if she wasn't happy with me, I was assured of that. What the neighbors were up to—it was really not my place. Even so, I felt for Mr. Knight. He seemed lonely, and even as grumpy as he was, I felt led to want to help him. Was he eating healthfully? Maybe someone could come in and clean for him?

I got in my car, put down all the windows to let out the oppressive heat and then put the car in reverse, looking behind and side to side before pulling out of the driveway. I stopped after crawling just a few feet. The Chrysler I had been following earlier was behind me, blocking the driveway.

CHAPTER SIXTEEN

Leon Knight emerged from the passenger seat after the car slowly moved forward, parking in front of the house next door.

A woman crawled out of the backseat and slammed the door. "I've just had it!" she exclaimed. She looked pissed. Then she noticed me still sitting there in the driveway gawking at them. "Hey, there's that girl who was looking for you last week." I could hear her say from my open windows.

I punched the buttons for the windows to close and continued backing out, looking over my right shoulder to the street behind me. There was a bang at my window, Leon had followed the car along as I approached the street. Shoot, there was no elegant way out. At least, not without hitting him.

I rolled down my window again. "Hi again!" I said cheerfully.

Now, Trixie was right next to him. "Yep, that's her."

I gave them both a blank look, "Her who?"

"Were you looking for me?" he asked.

"Uh, no. Nope." I continued with the fake 'completely oblivious' look and pretended I've never seen her in my life.

"No, no, no … lady, you were asking about Big K last week. Right over there—" she pointed down the block. "Next street over. Said you knew him."

"Sorry. Not me. I gotta go…" I tried to continue my slow backward roll before his hand hit the door frame again.

"Stop! What are you doing here?" he demanded.

I looked at my mom's house and nodded like *duh*, "Visiting my mother. Now, I need to go. Excuse me."

"Why were you asking about me?" He wasn't moving anywhere.

"I wasn't." I thought I'd try a different tactic. "Oh, I did see your dad outside earlier and I helped him back inside, Leon."

His startled look was priceless. He knew he'd never given me his name and I could see his wheels spinning trying to figure it out.

"He really shouldn't be out in the heat," I added. "But, don't worry, I got him some water and made sure he was comfortable inside. I see what you mean about the dementia—he swears you're not his son."

Trixie glared at him. "Who is this woman?" I think I surprised her with my familiarity to his family.

He leaned in the window slightly—way more than I was comfortable—and with gritted teeth said, "I'll take care of my father. You stay away."

"Are you screwing her, too?" the woman screamed out and slugged him in the arm.

He moved his hands off my window frame, turned to her, and screamed, "Shut up, Violet!"

I took the moment to quickly close the window and back out of the driveway, leaving them to argue. I saw his arms raised out to his sides frustrated that I had got away. Then, in my rearview mirror, I could see that the black vehicle remained parked in front of the house. During the entire altercation, I completely forgot there was a driver in that car. No one had got out, and the windows were so dark that I couldn't see in.

Wow, that was uncomfortable and odd. What was his problem? More importantly—if he knows Trixie, er, Violet, is he Big K? And, if that's the case, he's a drug dealer? And, *what's he doing at Mr. Knight's place?*

My phone interrupted the swirling thoughts.

"Hi JJ!"

"Just calling to see if today would be a good time to trim your mom's bushes?"

"Interesting timing. I'm just leaving her neighborhood. Had a very strange interaction with the neighbor and I'm basically escaping."

"What? Your mom's elderly neighbor?"

"That's just it. I'm starting to suspect that Mr. Knight has a visitor who is up to no good. I hope he's okay. Should I call and have the police do a wellness check?"

"Uh, well … I don't know the situation. Perhaps I could check things out when I trim your mom's shrubbery."

"Oh, yeah … that's why you called. I'm sorry. Yes, what time? I'll call her and warn that you're on the way."

"I'm available now. I'll head over."

"Ok, I'm headed back home. I'm sorry, I don't want any further contact with the man that just scared the crap out of me."

"No worries, I'll check it out and report back later."

We hung up and I headed home. I had thought about stopping in at work for a bit, but it was my day off and I really needed rest. By the time I walked in the front door, Shadow was crazy with energy. We went out back and she ran all over, getting her nervous energy under control. I threw her ball several times the full length of the yard so she'd run full strength.

"Hey girl, ready for some more *Bridgerton*?" I said in the high-pitched, get 'em excited voice. "Let's go binge!" She jumped up, as if giving me a high five. I laughed. She was such a character, and I seriously don't remember what I did before this sweetie came into my life.

* * *

The next morning, Shadow and I went for a jog around four-thirty. This time, we enjoyed the desert trails just outside of my development. After resting and achieving an amazing night's sleep, I had so much energy and the trail run felt great. Shadow seemed to agree. Usually when we get out of the neighborhood, I would take her leash off to go through the desert. Not this time of year. Snakes were out. She constantly wants to stick her nose in bushes, but I kept a tight rein on her and we did pretty good running along without any close calls. In general, I rarely actually see rattlesnakes, but I know they are hiding among bushes so I always assume they are there and I make plenty of noise so they'll stay away from us.

After a nice shower and breakfast for both of us, my phone started up again. First, my mother. Then, Alexis.

Mom asked me to check her cameras again. I did so as she told me the story of a man and woman climbing over the fence and they were *definitely* in her pool last night. She saw them this time. Scrolling through the feed, I saw there was an event detected, then it showed as offline for the next two hours. I went to each of the other two cameras and they also showed offline for that same period of time. Eleven-thirty to shortly after one in the morning.

"Did you look at the clock? What time was it?" I asked her.

"Clocks were flashing—not sure when they went out. But, my wrist watch said 11:42 p.m."

Interesting. Power went out. Why? There were no monsoon storms last night, but it has been awfully hot and sometimes our power grid can't keep up with all the air conditioners running constantly.

"Did you ask Margie if her power went out, too?"

"No, I haven't talked to her yet this morning."

"Ok. I don't see anything on your cameras, Mom, but it looks like the power may have gone out. You went and actually *saw* people swimming?"

"I looked out the bathroom window. Yes."

"Mom, the bathroom window doesn't face the pool."

"Well, um," she thought about it for a second, "I heard it. I know I did."

"Could it have been a dream?"

"No! Libby, you have to believe me!"

"Ok. I do. It's ok. Let's call the police and have them check it out, ok?"

"JJ was already here," she said matter-of-factly.

"Yes, he was … to trim the bush. Did he check out the cameras yesterday?"

"He spoke to the neighbor and yes, he secured everything for me. Said I was safe."

I'd have to talk to JJ to get more specific information. This was going nowhere.

"Ok, mom. Glad you're safe. I'll talk to JJ to learn what to do next."

I hung up and felt my frustration growing since it appeared she was imagining these things. I didn't want to completely discard what she was saying, in case it turned out she was right. However, I'm not very good with 'boy who cried wolf' situations. I tend to lean toward common sense and scientific proof rather than conspiracy theories. This was starting to feel like the latter.

That's when Alexis called. "Hello, my friend!" I answered.

"You are not going to believe this, Libs," she stated, "Sasha was followed yesterday by that guy in the black car! She was coming home from the doctor's office and was followed from Recker Rd. all the way till she was nearly home. Thankfully, she noticed and drove past her house and straight to the police substation—you know, over there on University."

I couldn't believe what I was hearing. Why would he try to contact her again—after the date gone bad and with the police looking for him? But, also, I couldn't stop thinking of the fact that it was a black car. A black Chrysler? That *is* what was parked in Sasha's driveway the night she was attacked. I'm not sure why I hadn't connected that prior to now. Could it possibly be the same one I followed just yesterday? The same as Leon and Violet got out of in front of Mr. Knight's house? Was Sasha's date the same person and could all this be related to drugs?

"Libs, you there?"

"Uh, yeah … I was thinking I didn't even know where the police station is. How did she know where to go in that moment?"

"Her navigation system."

"Ah, yeah. So, what happened?"

"He drove on. She never got the license plate. And, because he is clearly going by a different name, she really couldn't file a report that they could follow up with well."

"Different name? Did I know that?"

"Well, she told us his name was Russell … remember?" Vaguely. "Police told her they hit a dead end—no known Russell Kartwood in this state. Obviously, he signed up on that dating app using a fake name and played her along."

"So, they have no idea how to find this guy? Isn't there a way through the dating app they both are signed up on?"

"Well, I suppose theoretically, but not when the information he used to sign up was fake!"

"True. Wow! I'm so happy she was aware, didn't go home, and nothing bad happened to her. Holy crap! But, he knows where she lives … she needs to get out of there."

"I told her the same. I think she has called her aunt in California. I'm just praying she goes … before he shows up again."

"Anything more on Chester? Have you heard from Officer Lahey on that?"

"No, I'd think she'd contact you … but, no, nothing."

"Ok, I'll check in with her and let you know. You haven't seen him around the business again, have you?"

"No. Neither Bella nor I have."

"Good. Keep eyes open though. I'll be in later … I have appointments; three ninety-minute sessions this afternoon. I'll be in around noon."

"Ok, see you then!"

Once I hung up with Alexa, I felt compelled to take another drive. *I'm going to drive through that neighborhood off Southern again—just to see if I run across the black car that seems to be everywhere lately.* I was still baffled about the car that dropped off Leon and Violet yesterday. Was that a coincidence? Could these separate incidents have a connection? I was too curious for my own good.

On the way there, JJ called. I relayed what Mom informed me of this morning and he said everything looked in order at her house when he was there yesterday. The bush had been taken care of and he couldn't see any indication that someone had come through her locked gate. The lock had not been tampered with. Yes, someone could climb a six-foot block fence, but it was highly unlikely … especially, coming or going in swimwear.

"Was that black car still there when you arrived?" I asked him.

"No, but I did see the old man on the patio. He waved me over, so I went and we chatted for a bit. He said no one was there and I didn't hear or see any evidence of anyone else there. He also knew nothing of a confrontation involving you yesterday."

"Hm. That's interesting."

"Probably just family issues. I think you mentioned dementia too … I could see that."

"Ok. Well, thanks for checking out the situation. Maybe

I am just making something out of nothing. I'll leave it."

"Your mom looked great. We had a nice long visit. She's a doll."

After a few minutes of chit-chat, we both went on our way. I did not tell him I was surveilling a neighborhood and I'm confident that he actually believed I was going to drop it. Honestly, I'm not sure it's possible for me to let something go when my gut is telling me different. I'm on to *something* and I just need to flesh this out.

I drove the same exact route as I did when following the car yesterday. Up and down each street, slowly. It was middle of the day and very hot, so there weren't kids running around playing. Apparently, many people were home, but holed up inside their houses in the air conditioning—I could see at least one car in most of the driveways. I rounded the corner, and then accelerated down the last of the four side streets. When I got about half way down the street, I noticed someone had walked out from a yellow-trimmed modest home. It was a woman walking down the street in the opposite way I was traveling. When she got closer, I could see that it was Violet. Her face was red and swollen looking; she was obviously crying.

We were several houses away from the one she had walked away from when I pulled over and asked if she was okay.

"Are you just everywhere in this city?" She gave me a scalding look. "*Who are you?*"

I couldn't come up with an excuse for being in this neighborhood quick enough so I focused on the part of the question about who I was.

"Seriously, I was visiting my mother yesterday. I am there a lot."

"So, you're looking for drugs in the neighborhood your

mother lives in?" Suddenly, she got sassier, smacking her ever-present gum, hand moved to her popped-out right hip.

"Uh, well … no, not precisely." I decided I needed to get on top of the questioning here. I pointed to my eyes indicating I see her swollen face. "Violet, you've obviously been crying. Are you okay?"

My guess was that she wasn't used to people caring about her feelings because my concern made her well up again.

"I'm so sick of my life. Men …" she lowered her face as tears started to fall again.

"Is Leon your boyfriend then?" I asked cautiously.

"Nah. He's a putz—I'm so pissed at him. But, he introduced me to my boyfriend," she turned and pointed back toward the house she came from. "I thought we had something, but now I realize I'm just a whore to him." She wiped the tears from her face and looked back again, trembling.

Sensing she was afraid of something, or someone… "Listen, can I give you a ride somewhere?"

"You'd do that?" She blew a huge bubble. Her gum color of choice today was purple.

"Do you have a mask?"

She rolled her eyes. Then, after reconsidering, she pulled one from her skimpy jean skirt pocket. The mask was a hot pink fabric encrusted with rhinestones, the sun caught one and sparkled me right in the eye.

"I can see you're upset. C'mon." I indicated for her to go around to the passenger door. She climbed in as I put my mask on too.

"Thanks. It's so flippin' hot out today. You can just take

me to the bus stop."

"I'll take you wherever you're going—the buses are pretty uncomfortable this time of year too."

"I need to get to Leon's."

"Oh, perfect. Heading to my mom's anyway. Let's go!"

"Why did you pretend you never knew me?"

I stared at her blankly. Then, remembered the interaction with Leon yesterday. *Libby, think…quick!* "Uh, I guess I was uncomfortable now that I know he's my mom's neighbor. Thought I was flying under the radar. I was just looking for a little *something*—friend with cancer, you know."

Now it was her turn looking at me unbelievably. "You know you can walk into any dispensary now to get what your friend would need," she stated bluntly.

I am just not good at this impromptu stuff!

"Right. Keep forgetting. Thanks." Shifting uncomfortably in my seat, I wanted to know more about her boyfriend. "So, was that your boyfriend that dropped you off yesterday—black car?"

"Ah, yeah." She paused; I thought she was tearing up again. "He's been lying to me. I know there's someone else. I can't believe after everything…" she caught herself and looked over at me.

"How long have you known him?"

"Two months."

Oh, so not a long-standing relationship then. "What's 'everything'…"

"I don't know…" she looked out at the side mirror. "Shit! He's following us."

Oh lovely. Best I could figure, we have a mad boyfriend following us. The worst-case scenario was that we have an angry drug dealer following us. I'm not sure either scenario was one I needed to be part of.

She continued, "I've sold so much shit for him. He owed me!"

Looking over at her nervously, "Um, what are you talking about?"

She patted the backpack she was carrying. "I took what he owed me."

"And what's that?"

"Just a couple pounds of heroin…"

I choked. "Wha … *pounds? … uh, here* in the car?"

"Yeah, right here." She lifted the flap and showed me.

Shit was right. What on earth am I going to do now? I want no part of this!

I looked in the rearview mirror only to see the big fat chrome grill right at my bumper.

"Violet. How dangerous is he?" I continued monitoring my mirrors. There was no traffic immediately in front of me as we headed down Main St; I kept my eyes both on traffic and my mirrors.

"That's why I left," she started crying again. "He's terrifying. At first, he was so sweet. And soooo good in bed." She perked up briefly with a little wink. "He's changed though. Something happened a week or so ago. Now, he just uses me as a punchin' bag."

"What?!" My jaw dropped. Every bit of the conversation was making me more and more nervous. I kept looking out for police—*where are the cops when you need one?* "Listen, Violet. Let's get some help for you—*no one* should treat you like that." I turned onto Country Club headed north; I knew I could get to University without too much question about where we were going—it was still in the general direction of Mom's neighborhood. I was just praying that we'd lose him and I could make it to the police station.

She sniffled some more. "What do you mean? Like the cops or somethin'?"

I didn't want to alarm her so I kept it casual. "I have friends. We could figure out something safe."

She turned around to look behind us. "Not with him on our tail."

I was thinking about that too, but praying that he'd figure out we were headed to the police and he'd bail. My next problem would be her—there's no way she wouldn't flip out when I turned into a precinct. She has heroin on her. *Think, Libby. Think.*

"Hey, let me call my friend now. See if he's home … maybe he has a suggestion on how we can lose your, uh…" I glanced back in the mirror again, "erm, *friend.*"

She sniffled, pulled a tissue from her bag and wiped her nose. "Maybe I should just go back to him. As long as I don't sell this first," she glanced down at the bag on her lap, "I can convince him I was helping and I didn't steal it."

"Violet. He's going to beat the crap out of you and you know it. Let me help." I started fidgeting with my phone system controls on the steering wheel. Thank goodness my contact list didn't show 'JJ-Police', it was simply 'JJ'. I scrolled to his name, but before I selected it, she yelled out.

"No! Don't call anyone. That'll just make more trouble. You don't know him. He killed his family years ago—pretty sure it was over drugs, too!"

"WHAT!?" This day was progressively getting worse. Why did I offer this girl a ride?

"Please. Don't call anyone. Just take me to Lanky's.

He's the only one that K trusts."

Oh no! *Big K? Drug dealer Big K?*

CHAPTER SEVENTEEN

Oh crap! We're being followed by Big K. I don't even know who that is, but from Lahey's warning and Trixie's—er, Violet's—behavior now, this *can't* be good.

"Please, Violet," I looked again in the rearview. How he hadn't rear-ended me yet, I couldn't figure it out. "Let's call my friend and he'll help us out."

Her eyes were as wide as saucers. "No police, right?"

"No police." Ok, I lied. But, what choice did I have? "However, we're going to have to fake out Big K and *pretend* to drive into the police station. He won't follow us there. We'll just wait a little bit and then I'll get you over to my friend. Sound good?"

She gave a little nod and didn't take her eyes off the side mirror. Thankfully, I was already headed to the station and we were nearly there. The black car was so far up my bumper that I cringed when I quickly made the right-hand turn into the precinct. By the grace of whoever watches out over me, he missed hitting us. He swerved hard, almost hitting another car next to him. Thank goodness, he kept traveling on down the street.

I pulled into the parking lot and went to the first empty space closest to the front door. Violet looked like a cat who was just about to get a bath—ready to claw me and run.

"It's okay," I tried to soothe, "we're not going in. Trust me."

I turned off the car so I could use my phone without the whole conversation being heard over the car speakers. *Please answer JJ.* My eyes scanned the parking lot, and more specifically, the driveway we just turned in here from. No black car—good.

"Hey, bud! Need some advice *now*, can't have the police involved." I just prayed he understood my impromptu code for 'cop role needed to be put on pause'.

"Sure, Libs—what's up?"

"I have a *friend*. She's in a little trouble and I wanted to see if we can *help* her." Each word was deliberate and slow. Violet looked at me as if I was a moron. I kept an eye on my rearview mirror, certain I was going to see a black car or a mad man running at me ready to bash in my windows.

"Where do you want to meet?" he asked.

"Our business?"

"Be there in ten."

That was easy. I was fairly certain he caught on to my troubled voice. Now, I just prayed he didn't call in for help. Last thing we needed was to have a huge show of red and blue when we pulled up in front of my business.

"Ok. Let's go meet JJ. He's cool. You'll see." She didn't

look so sure and I wasn't convinced that she still wouldn't leap out of the car and flee.

I realized it had been a while since I had taken a deep breath. My heart was still slamming into the side of my ribcage as I looked all around the parking lot for trouble. I started to back out carefully once I was convinced that we were in the clear. Instead of heading in the same direction we had taken to get here, I decided to drive the opposite way first. Then, I took some neighborhood streets to wind my way to the next major artery that would lead us to the spa. All the while, my eyes were casing the area. So were Violet's.

By the time we turned into the parking lot at my business, I was assured that we were not being followed by the black car. I could see that JJ was already there. It was then that I realized Bella, Alexis, and a client were in the building, too. I was taking an unpredictable drug dealer in there. Was this the smartest idea? Too late now. We got out of the car and continued to look over our shoulders all the way inside. Violet was holding tightly to her bag.

"C'mon. It's okay. Need to get out of the parking lot." I hurried her along as it seemed like she started to hesitate.

When we got inside, I just rushed Violet through the lobby, around the front counter and directly to the back office—without even greeting Bella. Alexis was in her therapy room with a client so we had the place mostly to ourselves—or at least, Violet would think so. JJ was sitting in the office and lifted his head from his smartphone as we walked in.

"Hi, JJ. This is Violet. Can I have a quick word with you?" I pointed to the Serenity room. "Out there. Violet, please take a seat, we'll be right back."

We walked into the Serenity room, leaving the glass doors open where we could see right into the office. I still wasn't convinced she wouldn't run.

"Who is that?" JJ whispered.

Turning my back to the door, I mouthed, "Violet is part of that drug ring!"

"How do you know? No, more importantly, how are you involved?"

"I'll tell you later. For now, just go along. You are *not* a cop. We can't scare her off. She needs protection from Big K."

His eyes grew wide. "Big K?!" His head spun around, looking in all directions as though the drug dealer may have overheard.

"Yes. This is his *girlfriend*. Pretty certain she's a prostitute, but never mind that for now. That bag she has..." I lowered my whisper even further and again mouthed, "... *drugs!* Heroin."

"Libby! What?!"

"Ok, ok. I know. I'm in over my head. This is why I need your help. Your phone—set the recorder app. Let's go learn more..." I signaled for him to go first through the doorway.

He did as instructed, but he wasn't very happy about it.

* * *

Violet spilled it all. Lanky convinced George Knight that he was his son. At least, at first, George bought it but that had since changed so Leon started giving him a mild sedative to keep him groggy. Lanky was a drug runner for Big K and used his newfound home as a base. Yes, they steal from unsuspecting elderly people and sell the goods for more money. In addition, they ride from that neighborhood to Main St. where most of their sales occur. Big K has a wide network of runners in Mesa—all the way from Center St. out to Power Rd.

The most shocking thing I learned was that Leon and Violet *have* been freaking out my mother. It was Leon's idea. He thought that if he could get George and Julia into nursing homes, then he'd buy the two houses and have that entire corner to run his operation without nosey bodies around.

"But, it's a 55+ community … he wouldn't be allowed to buy there," I pointed out.

"I never said he was smart!" she laughed. "He's a complete idiot. I had to point out to him that he needed to shut power off to those cameras or we'd be caught in the pool. He never even saw the cameras. Idiot!"

After a couple hours of divulging everything she knew about Lanky and Big K, JJ stepped out to use the restroom.

"Why are you telling us all of this now?" I asked.

"I never meant to become so involved. This isn't me. I entertain men, but I'm not a drug dealer. Last night Big K scared me worse than any mean trick I've ever had." She leaned forward, very pointedly she said, "He is pure evil. The only reason I'm alive right now is because I laced some of this," she pointed to her package in her lap, "with fentanyl and he crashed."

"Why didn't you leave right then … last night?"

"Well, it was very early morning by the time he passed out … I got scared. Thought I may have killed him. I waited around to be sure he was breathing. I wanted to stop him from hitting me, but I didn't mean to *kill him*. I left when he began to stir—just before you found me walking down the street."

I've never understood this lifestyle so it was difficult to identify with her plight. However, any woman getting beaten for whatever reason—I would help them.

"Can I get you some water? Tea?" I asked her.

"When are we going to the safe house?"

JJ walked in then. "In a little bit. I need to get that secured. Can I see that heroin?" He reached out to the bag that she continued to hold tightly to her.

She eyed him suspiciously. "This is mine."

I reminded her, "You don't want to be a dealer. That's what you just told me."

She squirmed in her seat, then looked up at JJ again. "He's going to kill me." Her eyes watered and she hesitantly lifted the bag and handed it to my friend. "What are you going to do with it?"

He just turned and left. She looked over to me panicked and wild-eyed.

"He's calling the cops, isn't he?" Her head spun around and she leaped out of the chair, springing out of the room like a gazelle. I followed her.

"Violet!" I yelled. "Wait!"

I caught up to her at the door to the front desk. Bella accidentally opened that door right into Violet's face. She fell to the floor writhing, her hands covering her nose.

"Oh no! I'm soooo sorry!" Bella was already kneeling down to see if she could help.

Through the door, I saw several police officers in the lobby. That's where JJ had gone earlier—not to the restroom. Violet was bleeding from her nose and the gash on her forehead. I grabbed some tissues from a box nearby and tried to help.

"Dammit!! I knew I couldn't trust you!!!" she screamed in my face. "Just like your nosey mother, too!!"

JJ stepped in and helped pick her up off the floor. "Trust me, you are safer where I'm taking you." He cuffed her and hauled her out to the police car.

CHAPTER EIGHTEEN

"What do you mean they got away?" I shouted into the phone as Office Lahey was trying to give me an update the next morning. "You guys know what car they're in!"

"Do you understand how many black Chrysler 300s there are in this metropolitan city area? I'm sure they understood that Violet was going to spill her guts when you guys pulled into the station. Big K probably immediately went to get Leon and they could be in Mexico by now, for all we know." Lahey sighed in exasperation.

Calming down a little because I did understand it's not that easy, I asked, "What's going to happen to Violet?"

"So long as she cooperates with us and helps us find the others, I'm sure the District Attorney will go easy on her."

"Ok, so now we know who has been messing with my mother. But, are these the same people who attacked Lexi and Sasha? I'm not convinced it is. And, if not, then who?"

"Exactly. We're still working on it."

Patience is not something I had right now. It shouldn't be this hard.

After the call with Officer Lahey, I headed to work and then planned to stop over at my mom's after my two morning appointments. I wanted to talk to Mr. Knight. The police already had been there and, from what Lahey told me, it sounded like Leon had grabbed as much of his stuff as he could and ran. I wondered if there was anything left there that might indicate where he would have gone. Although, I'm sure the police confiscated anything considered as evidence.

Later that afternoon, I could see that Mr. Knight wasn't on his front patio so I knocked on the door. No sounds from inside and no one answered the door. I knocked again, but there was only silence so I headed across the yard and over to my mom's.

"Mom!" I yelled as I let myself inside with my key.

"In here, Libby!" I found her sitting at her kitchen table looking through some bills.

"Hey there." I gave her a kiss on her forehead and patted her shoulder. "How's Mom today?"

"Something big happened next door late yesterday." My mom's eyes got huge and she proceeded to tell me how she and Margie spied from her neighbor's front porch. "There were five cop cars, and then an ambulance came as well."

"Did something happen to George?"

"Well, they took him to the hospital. I'm not sure what happened. The police were there for a long time though. I never did see that younger guy."

"Mom, I have some things to tell you." I wanted to make sure I had her attention and that she was ready to transition from her story.

"What's wrong?" she asked.

"A lot has happened since I last saw you. That younger guy next door is a bad guy. He was scamming poor George and he and that girl you saw … well, they *were* pranking you. I guess the idea was to make us all think you were out of your mind so you'd sell the house and ultimately move into assisted living, or something."

"What on earth? I'm not losing it, Libby!"

"Oh, I know that now. And, Mom, I'm sorry I doubted some of the stories you told me. The girl who was with Leon, she told the police everything. All about knocking out power to turn off the cameras. Swimming in your pool. Scratching at the side of your bedroom window to scare you. All of it."

She sat there for a few seconds, stunned. "Wow. Why would they do that?"

"I'm not sure we can make sense out of a druggie's antics honestly. Supposedly, they wanted to drive you and George away. Doesn't make any sense at all."

"So, they are in jail?" she asked.

"Violet—the girl, she is. Leon ran off and they are looking for him still."

It dawned on me right then that with Leon on the loose, Mom could be in danger. Since I was the one involved in getting Violet arrested and blowing their cover, what if they retaliated?

"Mom, I'd like for you to stay with me or Jordan for a

little while. Just till they catch these bad guys."

"You really think they'll come back here?"

"I don't know, but I sure don't want to take the chance."

I called JJ and consulted with him. He agreed. But, he also reminded me that we still didn't know who had tried breaking into my home so Mom probably wasn't any safer there either. At least until we figured out who was targeting us and the business.

* * *

By evening, Jordan and I had helped gather Mom's belongings and moved her to their guest bedroom. She definitely would be safer at Jordan's—at least from drug lords. Hopefully, she wouldn't get the virus being around the kids. After she was all settled there, I headed home. I had learned where they took George and I wanted to talk to him.

"Hi George, this is Libby. We met recently. You live next door to my mom."

He sounded a bit groggy, but he responded right away. "Yes, Libby. How are you?"

"I'm sorry to hear you are in the hospital. Do you need anything?"

"No. They're going to release me in the morning."

"What happened? Why are you in the hospital?"

"That boy was drugging me, apparently. They're running tests and helping me to come off the sedatives. The police came to take him away—but he left just before they arrived."

"I heard about that. You weren't injured or anything, right?"

"Nah. But the police found me sleeping and were

worried because they couldn't wake me. Guess my heart rate and blood pressure were really low too."

"Well, I'm very happy to hear you're getting the care you need. Do you know where Leon went?"

"I have no idea. I don't even know who he was! I told you he wasn't my son!" Suddenly he sounded a little more agitated. And, just as I was thinking that this was the most coherent conversation I'd had with him.

"Yes, I learned that too. I'm sorry I doubted you before. What a con man that kid was, huh?"

"I'm just thankful he's gone."

We talked for several more minutes and then hung up. I was just thankful he was alright and the drugs hadn't harmed him. I promised to come by and visit once he was released. I felt like I needed to check in on him and make sure Leon didn't come back.

Now that Mom was settled in at Jordan's and I had learned that George was okay, I finally felt like I could settle in for the evening. Bella was at school. Shadow and I had played ball in the backyard for as long as we could stand the heat, and now I could enjoy a nice cool salad in peace.

Not long after I ate, rinsed off my plate and silverware, my phone rang. My heart sank. *I don't want to get dragged off into any other drama—I'm tired.* I glanced at the screen and saw it was Greg so I answered the call.

"Hey you!" I answered, with more energy than I'd had all day.

"You sure sound good. Whatcha doin'?" he asked.

"It's been quite the day ... *another* day full of adventure, but I'm good."

I proceeded to tell him all the drama that occurred and about the one solved mystery. And then he updated me on the fire situation in the mountains. It was now more than eighty percent contained, which gave me a huge sigh of relief. I really had been worried about him and all the forest service and firefighting personnel. Thankfully, this summer, they hadn't lost anyone and they were able to save all structures from being destroyed too. There are many years they can't say that and it's just heartbreaking.

"So, want a guest? I could drive down tomorrow morning … if you're up for company?" he asked with that sweetness in his voice.

"Yes! I would *love* that!"

Suddenly, everything looked up.

CHAPTER NINETEEN

The second I saw Greg, my worries melted. Finally, something else to focus on besides watching over my shoulder constantly. More than ever, I would love to get away and go on a long hike in the middle of the wilderness where it's cooler and away from everyone. Hopefully soon that will happen.

I excused myself from the conversation with Bella and Greg over coffee to answer my phone.

"Alexis, good morning!"

"Hello, my friend. Did he get there safely?"

"Yes," I smiled, looking over at the handsome gentleman sitting there talking to Bella. "We're just having coffee and then we'll head over to the office."

"Okay. I just wanted to let you know I'll be a little

later than normal. Sasha called so I'm going to join her for breakfast. She's still not in a good space."

"Sure. Anything I can do to help?"

"No, I don't have my first client until eleven so we're good there."

"Okay, give Sasha my love. I hope she's alright."

Once I hung up the phone, the three of us finished our coffee and smoothies before heading off to work. We had already decided over the phone last night that I would give Greg his first Ashiatsu massage today since I didn't have another client until later in the morning. This way he could enjoy some time in the relaxation room when my client showed up and before we set out to do other stuff. He was unsure about massage—never done it before. I'm fairly sure he'll change his mind after receiving Ashiatsu.

Greg used the facilities at the spa to shower and change into one of the soft fuzzy robes that we provide to our clients. I led him into one of the therapy rooms after he had the opportunity to relax and do some deep breathing. With the lights dimmed, the citrus-blend essential oils steaming from the diffuser, and soft easy listening music piped into the room, we were ready to begin.

I explained the entire the process—it is a bare foot massage, so I stand on the table, but not physically on his body. Using my feet, I perform many of the same type of strokes on the major muscle groups as I would if I were using my hands and arms. After applying the oil all over his body with a brush, I climbed up on the table.

"Comfortable?" I asked.

"Very. I won't lie, though, this is fairly strange…" His chuckle was muffled in the headrest.

"Just relax. Let me know if I go too deep or if anything is uncomfortable; otherwise, just relax and let go of all your tension."

He did just that and I swear at one point he may have fallen asleep. His body jerked a little and he snorted—I laughed. After his two-hour treatment, I left him in the Serenity room with a hot cup of lavender tea while I got ready for my next client.

Bella found me in the laundry room depositing the sheets into the washer.

"You should see Greg…I'm pretty sure he's asleep," she laughed. "I took the teacup from his hands so he wouldn't drop it. Look," she pointed out the door, "he's definitely got the best seat in the house."

I stared at my boyfriend admiringly. He needed this. Poor man had been working around the clock for weeks now. I just loved that he was finally able to relax and have some time off. Finding it hard to pull myself away, I gathered my next client who was now waiting and we headed into the next therapy room for a ninety-minute session. Greg was still sacked out in the oversized cozy chair when I emerged.

I headed up to the front desk—I swore I heard voices talking louder than we normally would do when clients are in the building.

"I need to speak to her NOW!" Violet slammed her fist down on the counter and Bella didn't know what to do. I walked through the glass doors and immediately Violet said, "YOU! It's all your fault!"

"Violet. What are you doing here?" I asked cautiously.

"I went to jail! You said no cops!"

Trying to determine what to say next, I took a deep breath, walked around the counter, took her hand, and led her to a nearby chair. Normally, I wouldn't want a confrontation at the front desk where other clients may observe. My client had already left, though, and Greg was resting, so I decided to just sit here and see if I could get her calmed down. Bella sat down in her seat and pretended to get busy. I just hoped she was getting 9-1-1 ready to connect in case this escalated too far.

"I'm glad to see you're out of jail, Violet."

Unsure, she just stared at me. Her shiny long black hair had been washed and was pulled back in a ponytail holder. She didn't have on any makeup, but she was smacking on a piece of bubble gum. Her trademark. Today, it was blue.

"Thank you, Violet. What you were able to tell the police was very valuable and they will be able to protect you." I hoped that was true.

"Help?! You really think they are here to HELP?" she yelled. "I have nowhere to go. Big K is going to *kill me*."

"Have you heard from either of them?" I asked.

"Nah."

"Do you know where they would go?"

She blew a huge blue bubble. "You a cop too?"

"No, Violet. But, we need to find them so you are protected."

That appeared to satisfy her. She just kept smacking the gum and blowing bubbles out of nervousness. Her knee bounced up and down excitedly.

"I don't know. There is someone Big K knew here that wasn't in the business. Maybe he helped him again?"

"What do you mean 'again'?"

She shook her head. "I dunno all of it. But, I'm pretty sure there's a bigger boss than him. Someone has to be helping them."

"Did he ever talk about any certain place he's from or

where he'd like to go someday? You know, like a home-town ... or the Cayman Islands, or something?"

"You sound just like the cops. No! I told them too ... all he needed me for was sex." She bowed her head and popped another bubble before sucking it back into her mouth.

I just nodded my head. I did feel for her, but couldn't truly relate to her situation. I mean, this is her line of business. What did she expect? She calmed down enough though.

"I do want to help find them," she said quietly. "I'm just terrified, though. He's *not* a nice man. Well, he is—as long as he's getting what he wants. He's going to murder me if he finds me."

"Let me talk to the officers I know. I can't believe they let you out with nowhere to go."

"Oh, they did hook me up at a 'safe house', or so they said."

I rolled my eyes. Why didn't she say that to begin with?

"Okay. Go there. Probably best not to be around me—you know, they're going to be after me too, right?"

She nodded and gathered her bag. That was the last I saw of Violet.

When I went back into the Serenity room, Greg was no longer in his cozy chair; he had gone into the changing rooms. I transferred laundry and wrapped up a few bits of paperwork before he emerged, looking completely refreshed.

"What was that ruckus about?" he pointed to the front desk.

"Oh, that was the prostitute who ratted out the bad guys," I said nonchalantly as though this was normal everyday conversation. "She is a little bit mad at me for getting her arrested. Personally, I didn't get her arrested—she was holding a *lot* of heroin at the time. *That's* what got her arrested!"

The look on Greg's face said it all. "I think you've glossed over a few things, Libby. Prostitute? *Heroin*??"

"All in a day's work, I suppose." I giggled, grabbed his hand, and we headed to the front door.

Alexis was just coming inside.

"Greg! So good to see you again, my friend!" She gave him an enormous hug and kissed him on the cheek.

"Great to see you too! How's JJ?"

While they got caught up, I asked Bella if she'd be around tonight and maybe we'd have a little dinner party. Just the Johnsons and our household—we decided on easy, we'd order pizza.

"How's Sasha?" I turned to my friend.

"Ugh. She'll be fine, but all this has been really tough on her. She's terrified everywhere she goes, and she's certain he has been following her."

"Hey, I'm curious … even after the two drug thugs ran off, she still thinks she's being followed?"

I could see that Lexi wasn't connecting the two and wondered why I was asking.

"Uh huh … last night coming home from the group therapy session, she was followed again. Just like last time, she drove straight to the police station instead of her house and the person following left. She reported it to the police and an officer followed her home and checked her house before leaving. I felt bad because I couldn't attend last night, or I would have driven her."

"Wow. Was it a black Chrysler again?" I was curious.

"Yes, she thought so anyway. It was dark and more difficult to see."

Greg realized now why I had asked about the car. "Wasn't it that same type of car that followed you the other day?"

I nodded. Alexis' eyes got huge. "You think this is the same person who is selling drugs in your mother's neighborhood?"

I lifted my shoulders. "I don't know. But, I'm not sure I believe in coincidence either."

CHAPTER TWENTY

That evening, we ordered Barro's and had them deliver two large pizzas—one with all veggies and extra garlic, the other with sausage, pepperoni, and ham—a leafy green salad, and three dozen hot wings. JJ brought a twelve-pack of his favorite Blue Moon beer; Alexis brought a bottle of Cabernet Sauvignon.

Shadow was in heaven with a house full of people. If she had her way, this is exactly how it'd be every single day—the more, the merrier. As I was pulling out plates and napkins, I could hear the squeals of laughter coming from the living room.

"Whoa! Keep the running to the backyard, kids!" I said, as I nearly got bowled over trying to get to the kitchen table with my arms loaded.

As we sat down and started to eat, I could feel the tension with JJ. He wasn't his normal jovial self. From the time they arrived, it felt as though he was avoiding me. Of course, with Greg around, I'm sure it was just the two of them getting caught up again.

"Bella, can you bring the wine bottle when you come back?" I asked.

Greg updated the rest of the friends on all the happenings up north. Bella informed us that she is nearing the end of her first session in school and is preparing for the practical exams. Alexis told a funny client story— the typical embarrassing situation where a client farts midsession.

"How do you handle that? I hadn't even thought of that happening…" Greg asked.

"Well, there's a reason we diffuse essential oils or burn candles!" she laughed. "By the way, how was your Ashiatsu?"

"*Loved it*," he exclaimed. "It's good that I don't live here, I'd go broke doing this all the time."

"You made him pay?" she turned to me.

"He insisted!" I wiped my face with the napkin. "I didn't even know—he strong-armed Bella." I said, laughing.

"Hey, I'm not going to take advantage. You both have a business to run and I can pay for my own massages." He reached over and took another piece of the meat pizza.

We devoured the pizzas, most of the salad, and about half of the wings. I couldn't believe it. As I was cleaning up, I realized that JJ hadn't said much, if anything, throughout dinner. When he walked into the kitchen, I touched his arm. "Hey, is everything okay?"

He nodded and walked back out into the living, taking

a seat in the chair next to Greg. Alexis and I finished cleaning stuff up and sat at the breakfast bar drinking our wine. Bella joined us after running with Shadow and Joshua outside.

"Lex, is something bothering JJ?" I asked her.

She swallowed her sip of wine and set the glass down, shaking her head. "I don't think so, why?"

"Oh, nothing. Just quiet at dinner." We both looked over to the men who were in deep conversation. "No, never mind. Look at how cute they are—fast friends, huh?" I raised my wine glass to my lips.

After about another hour, the Johnsons decided it was time to go. Joshua was starting to get cranky the closer to bedtime it got. We walked them outside and I went to give JJ a hug. I know he saw me coming toward the driver's side of their car, but he just hopped in it really quick and shut the door. Weird. He's been my friend for many years and I've never known him to not give me a hug goodbye. I just watched in wonder as they pulled out from my driveway. *What did I do to upset JJ?*

Bella seemed to pick up on my mood. "That was weird, huh?" she asked.

"Yes. You noticed?" she nodded her head.

Greg looked to the ground when I looked over at him.

"You know what's wrong with JJ! Spill it, mister."

"Let's go inside, Libby." He took my hand and we walked back into the house.

Bella headed for her bedroom and Greg and I sat down on the sofa. All of a sudden, I felt like I was in trouble. I couldn't for the life of me think what I did wrong.

"Libby, JJ might not get that promotion he's been wanting," he said gently.

"Why?"

"Well, his suspect is now missing again. They were on to him and ready for SWAT to move in on him. Now he's gone."

"Oh, no."

"And ... he's not happy that you got involved."

"What?!" My head spun so quickly to face him, I got slightly dizzy.

"I'm not sure myself. There was a lot he couldn't tell me about the investigation, but he doesn't like the fact that you are running down the drug dealers. And, I can't say that I disagree, honestly." He changed positions on the sofa, pulling one leg up underneath himself and turning to fully face me. His caring expression made him that much more handsome. "What are you doing, Libby? It seems dangerous. Drug dealers, prostitutes, and heroin? I really don't like it."

I took a deep breath, turned to sit cross-legged facing him too. "I'm not sure what any of this has to do with JJ. But, honestly, I was just helping my mom figure out the scary stuff she was experiencing when I kind of stumbled into the whole drug thing. I did not purposely seek these people out. I just wanted to prove my mom wasn't going crazy." I stood up, and began to pace in the room. Trying not to get mad at Greg, who had nothing to do with any of this, I had to think a minute. *What does all this have to do with JJ's cold case?*

"Listen, Libby. I don't want to upset you. And, I certainly don't want this to dampen our short time together. You just asked what was wrong with JJ and I have answered with all I know."

Pacing, I walked around the sofa, to the kitchen, poured

another glass of wine, and continued to wear a path behind the couch now. There was a part of me that was getting angry. I don't think it was directed toward Greg though. Why couldn't my friend talk to me and tell me he's mad? Or, more importantly, *why* is he mad?

Greg was craning his neck watching me go back and forth behind him. "Can you come sit down again, Libby?"

I did move to the front of the couch so he'd stop wrenching his neck, but I couldn't sit down. Now, Shadow was following me. She knew something was wrong and she probably figured as much as I was moving around that we might be getting ready for a walk. I just let her keep following—we both needed our steps today, didn't we?

I started mumbling out loud, "Black car … Sasha … Violet … cold case." Something wasn't connecting for me, but there was more to this story. There had to be. "Chester … vandalism … hate crimes."

"Libby, you're starting to worry me." Greg stood up. He came over to me, grabbed my arms, and turned me to him. "Are you involved in something more? I mean, JJ is working on an old murder case."

"I know. That's what I'm trying to figure out." I gave in and let him hug me. While in his embrace, I realized it wasn't fair for me to be consumed by all this when he only had one more day to spend here in town. *I'll find JJ once Greg leaves and get to the bottom of it. For now, my boyfriend is here in front of me and that's where my attention needs to be.*

I took his hand and led him to the bedroom.

CHAPTER TWENTY-ONE

Two days later, I was driving down the street thinking how I missed Greg already and how fast our time together went by. We had spent time with my mom and my sister's family—which pleased them to no end. Greg appeared to enjoy them as well, but I was still uneasy about all of them getting so close.

As Shadow and I walked into the front doors at Dharma Inspired Day Spa, I found my mom standing there talking to Bella.

"Mom, you don't have an appointment today, do you?"

"No, no. I was just over there at the grocery store and decided to pop in. There's horrible news in the neighborhood, Libby. Mr. Knight was found dead in his home last night."

"Oh no! I didn't realize he was out of the hospital. Do you know what happened?" I asked.

"Not for sure. Gossip is starting to go around, but I don't know how they'd know?"

"What's the gossip?"

"One neighbor says heart attack. Another said he heard he must have had a stroke. Doreen's sure the kid was back—thinks he was murdered!"

That got my attention. "Did she see Leon?"

Mom just shook her head. "Oh, I brought you some raspberries! They were on sale—aren't they beautiful?" she asked as she pulled them out of the bag.

My mind was still with Mr. Knight and not focused on the fruit, but I did remember to be polite. "Thank you. They do look good."

"Well, I've gotta go. Margie needs help getting ready for the next watch meeting." And away she went.

Bella stared at me. "Was that her next-door neighbor she was talking about?"

I nodded my head. Horror started to envelope me as I realized the men could be back in the area. I was very happy that Mom was staying with Jordan, but I couldn't help but wonder if it was safe for her to attend that block watch meeting.

Night had already descended by the time my appointments were finished for the day. I called Officer Lahey to inquire about several things: 1) status on Chester, 2) was she aware of Mr. Knight's death? and 3) had they made progress with finding Sasha's attacker? What I learned wasn't exactly encouraging. No, no arrests for Chester Whitmore, even though I had seen him near my place of business after I got the restraining order. Yes, she was aware of Mr. Knight's death, and no, she couldn't tell me whether Leon was back in the area. And, finally, no … no further progress finding Sasha's attacker.

"But, Sasha was being followed! How can you not track that car?"

"She doesn't have a license plate number, Libby. I've told you, there are hundreds of that make and model around here."

"What about the charity he gave all those bikes to? Can't you learn something from those people—surely, they know who he is?"

There was silence on the line. "I don't know what you're talking about."

"Didn't Sasha tell you about her first date with the creep?"

"Uh, no. Maybe we need to follow up with her?"

"Yes!" I couldn't believe this. Why hadn't Sasha told them this? It could lead them directly to him!

We hung up and then I waited in the relaxation area for Alexis to finish so we could walk out together. As I sat there drinking my tea, enjoying the looped tracks of spa sounds, I started dreaming of taking time off to get back in the mountains for some hiking. It would be so nice to take a week or more for vacation. On one hand, I was thrilled that business had taken off and we were booking massage sessions out for weeks. However, that didn't lend well to taking a vacation. Alexis and I had discussed bringing in more help. There was a program through the school we attended where massage businesses could mentor new students. They worked on getting their hands-on practical hours for certification. I needed to call them and see if we could get that started—who knows, maybe we'll find good help that way?

Alexis walked out of her therapy room just then. Shadow ran over to greet her.

She reached down to my soft black pup, "Hey, girl … well, aren't you sweet, greeting me!" Lexi looked over to me, smiling wide, "As soon as I see Ms. Smith out, I'll be ready to go. Thank you for waiting."

"No worries. I'm just enjoying my tea." As if to prove the point, I held up my oversized blue mug with the intricate and colorful Mexican artwork displayed.

A few minutes after Alexis walked into the locker room with her client, the chime from the front door sounded. Shadow's voice was loud. I jumped, spilling some tea on my lap. *Hadn't I locked the front door?* I quickly set my mug on the side table and moved toward the front. I could see the shape of a person through the frosted glass door. My heart started to pound, my eyes shifting fast and surveilling the room for something to use as a weapon. There was a broom just inside the office door, so I ran and grabbed it. Shadow looked at me with a question in her eyes.

As I proceeded closer to the glass doors, I held the broom handle out in front of me ready to skewer the person who was not invited in. The person's shadow moved closer on the other side of the door. I could see a hand reach out to push the door open. Just as it opened wide, I swung hard and made direct contact with my assailant's head. The body went down hard as I screamed.

Bella?

Shadow immediately started licking Bella's face and nudging her.

Alexis came running from the locker room. "What's going on?"

I knelt down on the floor, holding Bella's head in my

hands, softly moving her hair away from her face and talking soothingly. Her eyes fluttered and she reached for her head, grimacing. I looked up at Alexis.

"I thought it was an intruder. I hit her with that broom handle—completely clocked her!"

With all of us on the floor now, Shadow sidled in closer to Bella's body; Alexis and I both checked her entire head for wounds and were like hawks hovering over her. She moved to sitting, pushing us away.

"I'm so sorry, Bella. I had no idea it was you. And, I thought I locked the door—oh man, I'm so jumpy lately!" My head fell forward. I felt horrible.

She wiped her eyes, touched her head again, and then looked me in the eyes. "We're all anxious since the break in, it's okay. Next time, I'll announce myself loudly," she smiled. "Wow, you've got a great swing, though!"

We helped her up and then sat her on one of the soft couches. I got her a cup of lemon infused water and we sat for a little longer.

"Should we go to urgent care—just to be safe?" Alexis asked her.

"I'm fine, guys."

"Okay. Let's go home. You need to rest for this evening." I wasn't giving her a choice. School or study groups could wait; she needed rest. Although she seemed much more alert and chattier again, I wasn't taking any chances.

Alexis and I closed everything up and walked Bella to her car. I followed her for the quick less-than-a-mile home.

Once we were in the house, and talked for an hour or so as we made dinner, I was confident she would be okay. We turned on the TV as we ate our chicken and vegetable pot pies hot from the oven. I wasn't even paying attention to the breaking news on TV, but then I suddenly dropped my fork, startling Bella and Shadow.

I just stared at the photo of the man displayed on the television. I felt sick to my stomach.

CHAPTER TWENTY-TWO

The perky TV reporter was saying, "Chester Whitmore, 55, from Mesa, was arrested this evening. He is the prime suspect in the rape and assault of seven women in the valley over the past year. It's unclear at this point if police believe he's the only assailant. This is breaking news but be assured, we will be here on scene to bring you all the facts as we get them. Over to you, Ron."

I ran to my bathroom. I was sweating, dry heaving, and my heart pounded heavily. I splashed cold water over my face and brushed my teeth. *Chester was the molester?* I couldn't catch my breath all of a sudden and I fell to the floor. I sat there, pulling my knees in closer and hugging myself ... rocking slightly for comfort.

Bella quietly tapped on the bathroom door. "Libby, you okay?"

"Mmm, hm. Come on in."

She slowly moved the door open and then crawled down on the floor with me.

"I just can't believe our client's husband is the serial rapist in the news. He's been at our place. How many times each of us were in danger ..." I was stunned.

My phone was ringing in the other room. Bella ran and brought the phone to me. It was Alexis.

"You saw it too?" I asked her.

"Saw what?" she replied. "I was just calling to see how Bella was doing. Also, JJ got called into the station—looks like there was a break in his case. But, what are you talking about? What did you see?"

"Chester has been arrested."

"It's about time!" she exclaimed. "I know he's responsible for the vandalism—and scaring us. About time he's being held accountable."

My words felt like sludge in my mouth; I could barely get them out. "No. Lexi. He was arrested for raping all those women."

There was silence.

"Certainly, he's not the one who attacked Sasha?" I asked. "She didn't describe him as having red hair, did she?"

"I can't believe this," Alexis whispered. "No, no, she described her attacker as having cropped black, or brown hair, I think."

We talked awhile longer and eventually I regained strength—at least, I no longer felt sick to my stomach. After finishing our conversation, Bella and I went back to clean up from dinner and then I soaked in a nice hot bath. My brain couldn't take in another single bit of information today.

* * *

First thing in the morning, I dialed Officer Lahey. She wasn't available so I tried Officer Talin instead. The call was extremely short—all she said was, "Get to our station right away, Libby." And I did.

I rifled through my glovebox looking for the new KN95 masks I stored in there. Once I put one on, I dashed up the steps to the station. Opening the double glass doors, I asked the front desk for Officer Talin and was led down a very long, white tiled hallway with bright white fluorescent lighting. It made me want to put my sunglasses back on. Instead, I found my eyes slightly squinted as I looked through the crinkled old blinds into the offices I passed. Eventually, I found myself in front of Officers Lahey and Talin, and to my surprise, JJ was in the room as well.

"Thank you for coming so quickly, Libby." Talin closed the door to the office and led me to an empty chair. JJ stayed standing, but the other officers took seats facing me. Officer Talin behind the desk. "Did you see the news?"

I nodded my head.

"I apologize that we couldn't fill you in on all the details earlier, but please be assured that we kept a tail on Mr. Whitmore—ever since your first complaint."

I nodded again. *Why was I here? She couldn't tell me that over the phone?*

JJ piped up. "Libby, Whitmore is connected with my cold case. You have directly led us to him, which now has proven essential to catching the man who murdered his family many years ago. He and Chester were friends, dating back to the '80s where they both spent time in a juvenile detention center."

My brain was trying to catch up. "So, why am I here now? You have him in custody."

"We want to set up a sting operation to catch Milo Robinson."

"That's the person you believed was hiding here in Arizona, but killed his family in Ohio?" I could feel my eyebrows furrowing as I still didn't fully grasp how this involved me.

Officer Lahey stepped in. "Libby, we're going to let Chester go home today. His family posted his bond."

I jumped up horrified, "What?!"

She continued, "Don't worry. Sit down, Libby." Lahey pointed toward my chair and I slowly settled back in. "We will continue to keep a close eye on him, trust us. Chester is not the one we're concerned about."

"How can you not be concerned? He *raped* women!" I couldn't understand.

"He is a registered sex offender—that's true. It's *possible* he may be involved, but we don't have conclusive evidence of that yet. He doesn't know that. The media doesn't either. He maintains his innocence *and* he is willing to help us find his friend." Officer Lahey stood up and walked to a small refrigerator in the corner. "Water?" she asked us collectively in the room. We each took one.

Talin spoke up and continued, "Whitmore and Robinson are cohorts. We are fairly certain that Whitmore is directly responsible for hiding Robinson—aiding a fugitive. He understands that will get him more time. It's been tricky to gather direct evidence to date; however, by getting his cooperation, we're confident we can finally solve this."

I turned to JJ. "Is this all related to Violet and the drug gangs?"

He shook his head. "At one point, I thought it was. However, I think I was wasting my time ... that path has run dry."

"How am I supposed to help?" I couldn't imagine.

Officer Lahey was quick to answer. "First, whatever we talk about today—it's just for those of us in this room to know. Don't say anything to Bella or Alexis. We don't want to concern them and the fewer people who know, the better." She looked over to Officer Talin and gave a short nod.

"Don't worry, Libby. I know it sounds scary. Your role will be very limited, but we felt we needed to bring you in on the plan so you and your friends don't get hurt. We promise we'll have the full force behind us and we are here to protect you. Now, here's how you're going to help...." All three of them moved in closer, speaking quietly, fully intent on all the details.

* * *

My heart rate hadn't slowed since I first took a seat in Officer Talin's office about an hour earlier. It had been weeks since all the drama started: at our place of business, at home, at my friend's home, and in my mom's neighborhood. All of it made my head spin, but one thing was for sure—if the police thought I could help trap these men, then I needed to pull up my big girl pants and be brave here. First and foremost, I wanted to get back to a 'normal' life and stop looking over my shoulder all the time. Whatever it took, I would trust the plan the police officers shared with me and I was ready to carry out my part.

And, mum's the word. I will carry on as though everything is 'normal'.

CHAPTER TWENTY-THREE

Sage, my client who lives out at the base of the Superstition Mountains, had convinced me to come to her home for a mobile treatment that afternoon. I loved going out to her place—even with the summer heat and dryness of the desert, the landscape surrounding the Superstitions was magical. This afternoon, there were monsoon storms in the forecast so it was also highly probable that I'd get to experience the mountain storm. She always talked about them. The ferocious thunder and lightning, echoing off the rocky canyons. The sweet smelling, rain-soaked desert sage, fragrant and practically singing after being soaked in the long-awaited nourishment from the clouds. Of course, I was always eager to make a house visit when my friend, Sage, called.

She showed me into her artistic space, where I set up my portable table and dressed it with the clean sheet coverings. This was routine for us and we fell right into comfortable conversation as I performed her treatment. She's been divorced now for several years, but has never been interested in marrying again. Sage is very independent, personable, and loving. Anyone would feel they've won the lottery being with a sweet soul, but she was content. That's why I was surprised when she started telling me all about her online dating stories.

From the micro-date—the one who told her he was nearly six feet tall, but showed up shorter than she was (under five foot five)—to the super touchy feely one, right in the middle of a restaurant. She had me giggling so hard with her stories. I almost forgot about the fact that I'm in the middle of a major operation with the police. It was nice to laugh with Sage and forget, for just a moment, that danger still lurked around every corner.

"...that's when I had enough and I asked him to leave."

"Did you feel you weren't safe?" I asked.

"He was a creep and I absolutely regretted inviting him to my home. I mean, we had several other dates prior—perfect gentleman. I don't know what happened." I helped her roll over onto her back, shielding her with the privacy sheet and adjusting the bolster under her knees. She picked up right where she left off. "I helped him load a bunch of bikes he was going to donate to a local charity, right here in AJ. He told many stories of his philanthropy and I just did not see the angry side until he came to my house. People are so strange."

The hair stood on the back of my neck.

"What did you say his name was?" I tried to keep the

alarm out of my voice.

"Russell."

As mentioned before, when performing massage, I can pick up on the feelings of my clients. And, occasionally, they can too. Thank goodness, this wasn't one of those times. I didn't want to ruin Sage's peace so I chose to stay quiet. For now.

She continued telling me more about Russell's philanthropy—the Boys and Girls Club seemed to be a favorite. St. Jude's was another one. Then, he helped out at various cities' soup kitchens feeding the poor. He sounded like a saint. I was fairly certain this is the exact same 'saint' who attacked Sasha.

We wrapped up the hour and a half massage and I stepped out to let her get dressed. As I stood to admire the red, rocky mountain, the storm clouds were building. The cloud-covered sun was a welcome relief from the intense heat earlier in the day. In the distance, I could see the rain already pummeling the hills, but it hadn't reached us yet. Sage emerged from the casita and stood with me, watching the winds starting to pick up.

"Sage, promise me you will never see that guy again," I pled.

She reached out and stroked my arm. "You sound so serious, Libby. He's just a punk. But, yes … I will promise. I do not want to go out with him again."

"I'm ninety percent sure … well, he sounds just like a 'charitable Russell' that attacked another good friend of mine. Please be careful. He nearly killed her."

Sage's face just dropped. The wind got much stronger and the dust was kicking up. She asked me to come inside and offered me some tea. We sat and I told her about my friend and the entire story as I knew it. I also gave her the number for Office Lahey—just in case. As I was getting ready to pack up the table, sheets, and oils, the clouds let loose and the rain poured onto the desert. We decided to have another cuppa while we let it pass. After an hour or so, the rain slowed to a sprinkle. Before I left, I gave her a huge hug and once again pleaded with her to not be in contact with that man.

I was nearly home when my phone rang. Alexis. She and Bella were wondering where I was. On the schedule, it looked like I had an appointment with Sage, but they were unaware that I chose last minute to go to her home instead. With everything that had happened recently, I realized I should have let them know.

"Thank goodness." Alexis breathed a deep sigh of relief. "I just heard that Chester was released on bond. Then you weren't here. I just imagined that Chester was out for revenge, or something."

"Yeah, I heard he was out. That's unfortunate." Of course, I hadn't heard this as a press release, but I wasn't allowed to tell her how I knew. "I'm sure he'll pay his dues once the trial comes around."

"I sure hope so!"

"Have you heard from Sasha this week?" I asked, trying to change the subject before my best friend saw right through me.

"Yes, she is doing so much better! We had group therapy last night and she really opened up for the first time. I think she's finally starting to see some breakthroughs."

"We should get together with her—girls' night out?"

"I'll see what I can put together."

We chatted a bit longer before hanging up. The worst part of keeping a secret is knowing that you're going to have to lie to your best friend and loved ones; something I'm terrible at, and never want to be good doing. However, I know that this is for the greater good so I'll suck it up and play along.

* * *

I decided to grab Shadow from home and then go check in on Mom over at Jordan's house before staying in for the night. It's just a few minutes out of my way—no big deal. When we arrived, I found them finishing dinner and Jordan was at the kitchen sink doing the dishes. The kids ran off with Shadow upstairs to the playroom, which left the three of us alone.

"I want to go back home," Mom whined from her seat at the table.

I moved closer, putting my hand on her shoulder. "I know you do. I'm sure it won't be long." I realized then that I hadn't asked the officers anything about Big K or Lanky's whereabouts. I assumed I'd hear if there was anything new to report.

"I miss the neighborhood—Margie and Doreen have called several times and I saw them at the block watch meeting, so that was nice. I just miss chatting between our yards. Or coffee on the front patio. Dressing up as ninjas in the night…" she smiled.

I let out a hearty laugh before realizing that I'm not sure she had referred to herself as a ninja before. I had. How did she know I had? I looked at her skeptically.

"Yes, yes. I know you think I'm an old coot—probably losing my mind. But, I'm not!" Jordan looked between the both of us as though she wasn't in on the joke. Clearly, Mom and I had been spending too much sleuthing time together. Or, at least, talking about the mysteries of the neighborhood. Changing the subject, Mom quipped, "So, when is that hunkalicious man coming back?"

"Oh, here we go!" Jordan chuckled along with Mom, she was definitely all in on this particular line of ribbing.

"I'm hoping very soon…" my voice trailed off thinking about Greg. I really did miss him. I also realized then that he's another loved one I'd have to lie to.

Jordan rinsed and wrung out the sponge, hung up the hand towel, and joined us at the kitchen table. They had convinced me to eat a little bit—I helped myself to a couple pieces of reheated fish 'n chips and swallowed it down with some iced tea. It was the first time since breakfast that I was actually hungry. Somehow, chasing bad guys is a great diet strategy; I've had very little appetite lately.

Mom piped up, "The one thing I did hear from Doreen was that Mr. Knight's death was definitely a suspicious one. All the talk on the block was about the kid that swindled him. Word is that the neighbor on the next block over—the one directly behind the Knight residence—saw someone of his stature lurking around in the alley between their houses. She called the cops, but by the time they got there, no one was around. Mr. Knight was crabby because they woke him up. Next morning, he was found dead."

"Mom, until we hear these facts directly from the police, let's not believe gossip." It did raise my suspicions though. Would Leon actually come back around? That seemed very stupid to me. *I suppose we aren't actually dealing with the most intellectual person on the planet though, are we?*

"Oh, Libby … always trying to be practical. You know that the neighborhood gossip has, so far, proved to be true. I believe my friends." Mom picked up her mug and got up to rinse it out in the sink. As soon as she dried and set it to the side, she said, "I'll use this cup later, Jordan. Don't move it. I'm heading to my room to read now; I'm tired."

"I'm heading out, too. I'll run up and give the kids hugs and try to pry my dog away from them." Before heading up the stairs, I checked my smartwatch; it was already seven and I wasn't sure how so much time had passed. Then, I glanced at my text messages—there were two from Officer Talin. My heart stopped.

Tonight's the night.

You know what to do.

* * *

I went home and let Shadow out and fed her dinner. She seemed quite exhausted from all the play with her cousins; now she snoozed at my feet as I dressed in all black and pulled my hair back into a ponytail. Had I known we'd have work to do tonight, I would have let her rest earlier instead of taking her to my sister's house.

From the officer's received intelligence, Chester is known to frequent a park in a part of town I'm not quite familiar with. Apparently, he's been known to troll for women, but all I could wonder is what type of woman is at a park after dark. Seems dangerous to me. Also, isn't it ironic that this man, who comes off so high and mighty using his born-again judgement against *my* profession, is the one who is the registered sex offender? And, he's possibly the valley's serial rapist, *and* thought to be harboring a fugitive? What a piece! Anyway, my job tonight is to walk through a park at night. Seems simple enough. And, no, I won't be alone—first, Shadow is always my protector, plus, I've been wired to the hilt and assured that we have undercover officers located at various points throughout the park.

We loaded into Trina and drove out of my neighborhood, heading north on Power Rd. to the Loop 202 Red Mountain Freeway. Exiting on Country Club Dr., we drove south to 8th Ave. and made a right, then after a half mile or so, we took another right on Extension Rd. Trying to ignore the pounding against my ribcage, I chose a parking spot at the southeast end of the park. I looked around—there was a beat-up red sedan and an older four-door Buick, but those were the only vehicles I saw.

I got out of my 4-Runner and opened the back door to retrieve Shadow. Her tail was wagging uncontrollably; this was not a normal part of our nightly routine. Just as she was jumping down to the ground, a man's voice sounded loudly in my ear. I jumped, bumping my head on the doorframe as I spun around.

"Libby, can you hear me?" It was JJ coming through my earpiece.

"Shit! You scared the hell out of me, JJ!" I whispered.

"Sorry. See the red car?"

"Yep."

"That's me."

"Good cover."

"Stop looking over here! Just bend down and give Shadow some love," he instructed.

As I loved up my pup, he let me know that there was an unmarked police van on the opposite side of the park with several officers, including Talin and Lahey. In addition, there were undercover officers throughout the park that I'd never recognize as police. I was to just walk Shadow through the park without engaging with anyone. I could sit on benches, try out playground equipment, but not go into the restrooms or anywhere they couldn't directly see me.

"Got it."

I closed the car doors; Shadow and I set out nervously into the blackness. There were a few lights here and there, mainly surrounding the kid's playground, but otherwise, my eyes were having a hard time adjusting to the darkness. Whipping around side to side instead of in a straight path, Shadow was sniffing everywhere. Her tail wagging as fast as it could, she kept looking back at me as I imagined she was saying 'thank you for bringing me here, Mom'. I kept looking over my shoulders certain someone was about to grab me. No one was around that I could see.

"This seems pointless. There's nobody out here," I whispered, facing my mouth downward in case anyone was out there and observing me talking to myself.

"Just keep walking," JJ's voice was smooth and comforting.

Talin spoke up, "A black sedan just pulled up along 6th Ave. Two males headed into the park."

"Plates?" JJ asked.

"Can't see from where we're at, but we'll get it."

Shadow's ears perked up. Some small critter scurried across the grass in front of her. She watched it with curiosity until it ran off. Thank goodness I was not pulled along on a chase. We walked all the way to the other side of the park; I could see the van now, but I was careful to just ignore it. From everything I could tell, it was a slow night at the park. I wondered if there were busier weeknights vs. others. That's when I saw two men to the south of where we were. There was a bench near us, so I slowly sat down and pulled Shadow in close to me. She didn't bark and we both remained still as we watched the two dark figures.

They were walking fast—toward the restroom building near the center of the park which sat slightly higher on a grassy knoll. There was something very familiar about the tall one. In the darkness, I couldn't see details, but I could tell he was wearing a dark hoodie. Considering the temperatures were still in the high nineties, I couldn't imagine how anyone could wear extra clothing during the summer. Of course, I was glad that I chose all black— lightweight long sleeves, jeans, and black tennis shoes. We blended into the night and I don't think the men crossing the park now had any knowledge of our presence.

I whispered into my hidden microphone, "We saw two men about twenty yards away from us. Pretty sure they headed into the bathrooms. Want us to follow?"

"No!" JJ was quick to answer.

"Then why am I here?"

"Just stay there, Libby. We're hoping Chester will show up next."

"Ok, but you could have done all this without us." There was no further answer. I really wasn't trying to be a smarty-pants, but I felt it was a legitimate question.

"Talin. Team two is ready." An unfamiliar voice was loud and clear in my earpiece. "Just say when."

Talin's command was clear. "Hold your position team two."

Just when it felt like an eternity had passed, the two men came walking out of the bathrooms and proceeded in the direction from which they originally came.

"Team two. Go!" Talin shouted. I jumped, not expecting the command.

Shadow started barking and lurched forward, pulling my arm before I yanked her back. I could see four dark figures running. The two men took off and one fired a shot. I fell flat to the ground doing my best to pull Shadow with me. Even though they were headed in a different direction, I was afraid of an errant shot finding us.

"We got 'em!" I heard a male voice shout. There was a lot of static and shouting coming across the hot mic so I wasn't sure exactly what was being said, but Shadow and I got up and ran that direction. I could hardly hold her back.

The van doors opened and several officers headed to the scuffle, while a couple others ran for the black sedan nearby in the parking lot. Shadow and I went for the van where we found Officers Lahey and Talin.

"Was it Chester and the fugitive?" I asked breathlessly.

"Unfortunately, it wasn't." Talin answered. "But, one of them fired a shot at an officer. They're going downtown."

"Why did you think Chester would come to this park tonight?"

Team two was bringing the cuffed men to the police cars that had assembled near the van. Once they got closer, I could see their faces more clearly. One of them I had never seen before. The hooded guy turned toward me. *Lanky?* He sneered at me and Shadow, then spit on the ground. His nose and mouth were bleeding. His eyes bored into mine. A shiver ran from the top of my neck all the way to my groin. I hope he stays locked up, because his look spelled retaliation.

CHAPTER TWENTY-FOUR

It was an excruciatingly long night, and I never got my answer about why they thought the fugitive would be at that particular park or why Shadow and I walking through was considered an important part of the operation. I guess amateurs like me aren't privy to information like that. Still, I was curious and I was asked to hang around the station as they questioned all of us.

I had just gotten up to get a bottle of water from the vending machine when I saw Violet enter the station. She walked in, turned down another hallway away from me, but I knew it was her. Why was she here?

Officer Lahey approached us; Shadow startled awake and then started wagging her tail as Lahey bent down to pet her.

"It's been an awfully long night for you, hasn't it?" She cooed at my puppy. Yeah, she's worried about how long it's been for the sleeping dog, but what about the human sitting in this hard chair for hours? "Just a little bit longer, they are almost ready for you. Promise." Okay, her eyes showed a little bit of sympathy. I still think Shadow got more love, though.

"I'm not sure what more I can give them, other than what I said through the wire. You guys record that, don't you?"

"Yes, we do. But, the captain likes to get a full debrief in case you remember anything new."

"Was that Leon Knight—or whatever his real name is?"

"Yep. Drug deal. And, although he is a fugitive … he wasn't the one we were after tonight."

"Who was with him? Was it Big K?"

"Nope. Some young kid … he's not speaking so we're still trying to figure that out."

"And, why did you think …" Just as I started my question, the captain came out. He was ready for me now.

An hour later, Shadow and I were finally released and on our way home. I couldn't tell the captain anything new. I really hadn't seen anything that the other officers hadn't already observed. Even if I had, I'm not sure how my brain was supposed to function at three in the morning. This whole thing seemed like a crazy colossal waste of time to me. Both my dog and I curled into our beds and crashed until mid-morning.

* * *

The shrill of the phone ringing set my heart racing. My mind was foggy and it took a second to remember where I had set the phone down earlier.

"Libby, are you okay? Were you sleeping? It's ten thirty!"

"Alexis. I'm sorry. I meant to leave you a message and let you know that I wouldn't be in this morning; it's been quite a night." It was then that I remembered I couldn't really tell her why.

"Oh, honey, are you ill?"

"Not feeling stellar, but just needed some extra sleep. I'll be fine." It wasn't a complete lie; I didn't feel great after such a long day yesterday. "My first appointment is at two this afternoon. I'll be in well before that. Promise."

"Sounds good. Hey, Sasha said she'd be up for lunch. Maybe tomorrow?"

"Sure, that's sounds like a plan."

I rolled out of bed, headed to the kitchen to make coffee, and then let Shadow out of her crate to go outside. Standing in the backyard, I watched Shadow patrol while I took some deep breaths and stretched. The fog was lifting from my brain. As I was headed back inside, I realized something … I walked to that end of the house—the laundry room window was smashed in! I quickly went in through the sliding glass door and ran to the laundry room. Glass was *everywhere*. I turned and started dashing through the house checking each room. Nothing looked disturbed. I opened each closet, looking for evidence that someone had broken in. Bella was already gone to work for the day and nothing in her room looked out of place either. *When did this happen?* Surely, if a window broke during the night, one of us would hear it. I picked up my phone.

"Bella! Did you see the laundry room window?"

"Oh, gosh … Dangit, I meant to send you a text message. The kids next door—batting practice in their yard, a ball flew over and broke your window. The parents came by … they will pay for the replacement."

My heart slowed down. I could breathe once again. "Thank you. I immediately went to the worse-case scenario. Man, I'm jumpy!"

She laughed and then apologized again for not getting the word to me sooner.

Later that afternoon as I walked into my office, I gave myself the pep talk. Two hour-long massage sessions; I can do it! I was exhausted and really just wanted the police to catch all the bad guys so I wasn't constantly worried about what was around the next corner. There was good news—Leon was in jail and my mom could now go back to her home. However, Chester was out on bail and until he's back behind bars, I won't sleep well.

I still couldn't understand why they'd let him out. At least seven women raped in the valley in as many months. How does someone like that get the right to bail? I know, I know. He worked out a plea to help them catch the cold case fugitive, but still, I was not comfortable with him walking the streets. And, I wonder how his wife must be feeling? I believe Lahey had indicated she cooperated in turning him over to the police in the first place. Just as those thoughts were running through my head, I checked the computer for my first appointment. I like to read through a client's chart before they arrive so I am reminded of the work we did last time. When I pulled up the appointment, I saw

'Michelle Whitmore'. I ran up to the front desk.

"Bella, Michelle Whitmore ... really? She's my two o'clock appointment?" I was dumbfounded.

"Yes, she's starting up her membership again. Oh, Libby, that's another thing I forgot to tell you! I'm so sorry." Her eyes cast downward to the floor and she was shaking her head. "I don't know why I'm forgetting so many things recently."

"It's okay, Bella. I'm just really surprised. Since the arrest of her husband and all." I tried not to show the depth of my concern as I turned and headed back to the therapy rooms to get set up.

I can't imagine what I would talk about with a rapist's wife. And, the fact that he had targeted us and our business with threats. I'm not sure I'm comfortable with her in the building.

I completed all the finishing touches in the room and then went back to my office. I could see through the frosted doors that someone was already sitting in the relaxation room by the fountain. Alexis was at the desk.

"Was that Michelle Whitmore I saw come in?" she asked me.

My face dropped. "Yes. Unfortunately."

"Whoa, you're not comfortable with this, are you?"

"Not at all. Her husband threatened all of us in the past ... how do we know he won't come here today?"

"I see what you mean. But, consider ... she's not the problem. He is. Do you think she knew everything he was doing?"

"No. The police even confirmed that. She had no clue."

"Then, let's not punish her. A massage is probably exactly what she needs, right?"

"I guess I'd feel better about that if he were still in the

slammer. But, yes, you are right. Michelle's a lovely lady and I'll try to proceed as though nothing happened."

"Bella and I are here. We won't leave until you are all done." She smiled her radiant glow and I already felt better.

I quietly walked in through the frosted glass doors. I could see that Michelle had her eyes closed and was taking in the calm serene sounds of the crystal water fountain and the spa music. I gently tapped her hand that rested on a soft dusty-rose chenille pillow. She startled and opened her eyes.

"Hello, Michelle. Ready for your session?" I asked softly.

"Oh dear, I dozed a bit." Her expression turned to sorrow. "I'm so sorry, Libby. For everything. Thank you for accepting my appointment."

I didn't have to say anything. She stood up and I gave her a tight supporting hug and then we walked into the therapy room.

"Are we working on the same areas, or is something else bothering you today?" I asked her.

"Same issues—neck, upper back. And, mostly I'm here for relaxation."

"Very good. I'll step out of the room while you get settled. Face down to start." I stepped out and Alexis glanced at me from the office, asking if all was okay. I gave her the thumbs up.

When I stepped back into the massage room, Michelle almost immediately apologized for her husband once again.

"Well, I won't lie … I was very surprised to see your name on the schedule today. But, Michelle, I know that his actions are not yours. He's the bad guy. You are not."

"I had no idea, Libby. I swear!"

"I know."

"But, there is something that I want to confess. I need your advice."

"Okayyy…?"

"There's much I don't know about my soon to be ex-husband, and don't want to know. But, from early in our marriage, I knew about his best friend—he actually called him his 'brother'. We both heard about the tragedy with his family in Ohio. About a year ago, Ches started coming home late, leaving the house early. He said his work hours had changed and I believed him. Now, with everything I've learned from the police, I understand he wasn't at work at all. No wonder we never had any money." She took a deep breath and groaned when I kneaded deeper into her left shoulder muscle. "The thing that I forgot until recently was that I found some paperwork in the garage one day. Looked like a driver's license application—the name I saw was 'R. Kartwood'. The photo sitting near this paperwork seemed familiar, but I couldn't place it at the time. The more I thought about it, I wondered if it was the brother he'd spoken of? I never did meet him."

"Did you ask him about it?"

"I did. He just got very angry and told me to stay out of his business. It was work stuff. Whenever he was out of the house, I searched, but never found that paperwork, or anything else. I wished I had taken a picture of it."

"And, you didn't tell the police about that when he was arrested?"

"I completely forgot about it from a year ago. Plus, I don't think it had anything to do with why he was arrested."

"Then, why are you telling me about it now?"

"Actually, I'm not sure. Recently, it's something I always

seem to think about. You know he's out of jail, right?"

"Yes, I've heard. Where is he staying?"

"Honestly, I don't know. I had all the locks changed on the house. I really want to be someplace else, but the police don't seem to care about what I want. I can't believe they let him out!"

"So, you didn't pay his bond?"

"Fifty thousand!? Heavens no!"

"Do you know who did? The police told me it was family."

"No. But, again, maybe it's that 'brother'?" she questioned.

That sparked an idea. The police were willing for me to take part in a sting operation. So far, in my opinion, theirs was a horrible plan. I think I have something that would work far better!

"Michelle, I think you should tell the cops all this information. I do know that they think he's harboring a fugitive. It *has* to be the childhood friend. Has to be!"

She was silent for a moment. "What if he comes after me? I really just want the divorce to finalize and I want to move where he'll never find me."

"What if we put him away for life?" I added. The wheels were churning.

CHAPTER TWENTY-FIVE

Greg called the next morning. It had been about a week since we'd last talked and I definitely had missed his voice. The fires were out and now he was looking forward to having some extended time off work. That was terrific news, but I was unable to get away and wasn't quite sure when that would change. I told him what I could about the progress made with the investigation in my mother's neighborhood and briefly mentioned JJ was closer to solving his cold case. I wasn't going to fully go into that story because I still didn't know exactly how trapping Chester was going to solve JJ's cold case. We agreed that as soon as my schedule lightened up, we needed to do something big—a trip somewhere out of state, or even just a hiking/camping trip in Arizona. Didn't matter what, just so long as we could spend time together and get away from our jobs for a bit.

* * *

Several days later and everything was ready to set in motion. JJ and I had to fill Alexis in on the plan since it involved our business. I wouldn't say she was thrilled, but we all wanted to put this in the past, so we were willing to help out where we could.

Even though normally closed for business after eight in the evening, tonight we kept the 'Open' sign lit and all the lobby lights shined brightly. The sun hadn't quite set and the sky wasn't fully dark yet—still had about an hour of twilight before complete darkness. Bella was at school so Alexis sat at the front desk when Michelle walked in.

"Good evening, Michelle!" Alexis got up and gave her a big hug. While close to her ear, she whispered, "You ready?"

Michelle indicated 'yes' and then proceeded on through to the locker room where she changed into a soft robe and waited in the Serenity room for me to come get her. Alexis went back to the desk, looking straight outside where she could see the parking lot had already cleared out. From where she was sitting, she wasn't able to see the unmarked police van, but she was confident that JJ was out there somewhere and would come to her rescue, if needed.

I was in the back office where Officer Lahey was giving me last minute instructions and placing my wire. Officer Gonzales was with JJ outside, surveilling. Alexis, Michelle, and I all armed ourselves with items that could be used as weapons. Just in case.

"Which room will you be in?" I asked Lahey.

"The one at the end of this hall—we'll leave all therapy rooms open except the one you're in. Hopefully that way they find you before me. Don't worry, I can hear anything you say. If there is any sign of danger to you or Michelle, we'll be right here.

"Ok. You sure this is going to work?" With my question, she just shrugged and then left my office to hide out in Therapy Room 4. That did nothing for my confidence, but I walked over to where Michelle was already staged in Therapy Room 1.

"Libby, can you hear me?"

I confirmed, "10-4".

"Alexis?"

"Hear you loud and clear!"

"Ladies, hang tight. If Chester does his job right tonight, we'll have this all wrapped up in no time." Officer Lahey sounded confident now.

"I sure hope you're right," I added.

The evening dragged on as we went 'radio silent.' Michelle and I hung out in Therapy Room 1 talking, and Alexis had let us all know that she moved to her office with Shadow right at her feet. She left the front door unlocked, open for business. I looked up at the clock. It was nine o'clock.

Michelle was telling me all about the early days with Chester—they were so in love. She knew about his difficult childhood, but was impressed with how he'd found God and changed his life around. Many years went by before his controlling ways started. The way she told the story, she didn't even know when she became completely reliant upon him. When did he start dictating what nail polish or hair style she could have? She couldn't remember. As she divulged more, I learned that he forced her to be his alibi the first time the police came around. She started crying and I gave her a hug. The poor woman felt so guilty that she didn't stop any of those things. How could she, really? She explained that the more she pushed him toward confessing his sins at church, the more he resisted and stayed away from home. That was so unlike him and looking back, that's when she should have known. He wasn't the man she married. He had lost his way once again. She still felt led to stand by and support him, but she had no idea the extent of his crimes. I believed her. Hopefully the police would, too.

We all heard the front door chime. In my ear, I could hear JJ's voice, "Here we go!"

Shadow's bark was loud and ferocious. There was no doubt her bark was her warning one.

"Michelle!" the enormous booming voice sounded. "Where are you, Michelle?! Get out here now!"

I grabbed the nearby baseball bat. Instructed Michelle to get behind me as we sidled up against the wall near the closed door. We could hear stuff crashing outside of our door. I cringed, thinking of our beautiful place getting trashed.

Alexis' voice sounded calm. "I'm sorry, we're closed."

"We know she's here. Where is she?" This time I recognized the voice. It was Chester's. There were two men's voices.

"Just get rid of her!" the deep gravelly voice dictated. "And that dog!"

More banging around. A door slammed shut. I was quivering, standing there quietly. What have they done with my dog? Is Alexis okay?

Shadow's bark was fierce and loud, but I could tell it was more muffled. Must have been the office door that they slammed. We stood completely still, waiting for our door to open.

More barking and now scratching, too. Shadow was definitely locked behind a door and trying her best to tear it down.

"Milo, check the changing room. Over there!" Chester instructed.

"It's Russell, you idiot!" screamed the deep voice. "Now, where is that rat of a wife of yours?"

We heard the footsteps passing by our door. Just as the shadows crossed the threshold, Michelle let out a gasp. I turned and tried placing my hand over her mouth, silently asking her to be still and stay quiet. Tears were streaming down her face; she was having a difficult time. As I turned back facing the closed door, I detected a shadow in the sliver of light that shone through at the floor.

I raised the bat, ready to swing. I was sweating profusely and my hands were shaking. A few seconds passed, but it felt like an eternity. The shadow went away. Footfalls sounded as though the person was headed toward the locker room.

I took the moment to breathe. In my ear, Lahey asked, "Where'd they go?"

I was terrified to speak at all, but whispered, "Locker room."

JJ's voice was next, "Alexis? You okay?"

She whispered, "Yes." Shadow's bark was still persistent

as she wildly thrashed at the door.

"You IDIOT!" The deep voice was screaming again. "Of course, they aren't in the bathroom! She's here for a massage, dumbass!"

Our door whooshed open and slammed loudly against the wall behind it.

I stood and swung as hard as I could at my target. "Aaaaaacckkk" or something similar screeched from my vocals as I connected solidly with his torso, even though I had aimed for his head. He didn't budge. As I prepared to swing again quickly, I could see that this man was a good foot taller than me and solid muscle. I went for his throat. He grabbed the bat and easily removed it from my grasp and threw it aside. Then he backhanded me and I fell to the massage table and rolled to the floor.

Stars filled my vision, but I looked up at Michelle. She had brought a fire poker which she was wielding like a sword. With no fear at all, the man reached over and grabbed her arm, pulling her closer to him and plucking the fire poker from her grasp. He tossed it aside; it rolled under the massage table.

"Hon, just come with us and it will all be okay," Chester said to his wife in his best soothing voice. She was thrashing around as hard as she could to break from this behemoth's grip.

"I thought we were going to kill her to shut her up?" Milo sneered at his cohort.

Michelle's eyes opened wide and tears started to pour again. "Chester? What…"

"Shut up!" Chester screamed. Looking directly into Milo's eyes, he went berserk, his eyes wild and face redder than his hair. "It's all because of you that we're even here.

She's not the problem," he spat and poked Milo's chest with his finger. "The problem is that YOU were *supposed* to stay out of sight because YOU are the one who killed your family and are on the run. YOU needed to stay out of our business."

The large man suddenly dropped Michelle. She scooted over to me and we hid behind the table. He bumped chests with Chester, "Oh, you think you're so tough now, do you?" Shoving him backward, out into the hallway. We bent down further and watched from under the table. Milo hauled off and smacked him in the face. "All of this is because you couldn't keep your dick in your pants!"

"That's my business! I helped you get a new identity and you go blow it by starting up a drug business … assaulting women! What the hell, Milo?"

JJ's voice in my ear startled me. "Libby, do you see any guns?"

"Haven't seen any…" I whispered softly.

"Alexis?"

With Shadow still barking, she whispered much louder, "I'm tied up. I didn't see a gun. Could have one though."

"Team, let's move. We have confessions. Let's move in while these yahoo's are fighting. Everyone else, stay low, hold your locations. Lahey, ready?"

"10-4" Lahey's voice was clear.

I braced and felt Michelle do the same.

"It's RUSSELL, you moron. You're blowing my cover!" He smacked Chester again and this led to them wrestling around on the floor.

We heard the police unit come through the front door, but it didn't appear that these morons were the wiser. They kept pounding on each other. Michelle and I stayed put under the table in our room, in case shots were fired.

"POLICE! Don't move!" an officer screamed as he entered from the locker rooms. "Hands up! NOW!"

Milo sprung up and ran fast for the back door. He pushed through as though it weighed nothing at all. Several officers, including Lahey, ran through the door after him. Two others cuffed Chester, who didn't put up a fight at all. They shoved him to sit up against the wall.

JJ opened the closed office door to find Alexis tied to her chair. Shadow sprinted out of the room and out the back door where Milo had run.

As JJ cut the rope off Alexis' wrists, he gave her a kiss on the head. "You okay, love?"

She reached up around his neck and gave him a hug. "I'm fine. My ears are still ringing from all the barking in close quarters, but I'm doing well."

From the massage room floor, we saw JJ's and Alexis' feet coming out of the office and toward us. She stopped in front of Chester. "Thanks for helping bring Milo to the police, but I hope you rot in hell for the terror you brought on me, my friends, and family." She pivoted and came to us. "I think it's safe for you to come out now."

We crawled out from under the table and used it to help us get up off the floor. I quickly embraced Alexis and asked about Shadow. Just then, the back door opened and Shadow bounded in and over to me. Several officers followed her, with a final officer through the door holding Milo's handcuffed arm and guiding him toward the same wall next to Chester. We heard the front door chime again, followed soon by a couple more officers leading Violet into the room. She was also restrained.

"Found this one lurking outside," the red-headed

officer said.

She was clearly irritated. "Big K—you said you'd bail Lanky out of jail!"

I was confused. "Big K?"

She pointed directly at Milo. JJ and I glanced at each other with the knowing look between friends. We *had* been on the right path all along.

EPILOGUE

In the following days, we got back to business. The heaviness that had weighed on me previously had vanished—knowing that all the bad guys were behind bars was such a relief. Greg came down off the mountain and stayed with Bella and me for several days, which also eased my mind.

"Hey, sweetie, are you about ready?" Greg called to me from the living room.

"Just about. Can you take Shadow out?" I shouted.

I finished applying my makeup, drying and curling my hair, and now I closed the straps on my high heels. I looked in the mirror one last time and mused that I couldn't remember the last time I put on makeup or heels. I think it was at our grand opening. It's very rare—but I'd say that paying respects at someone's funeral qualifies as a valid reason to get all dolled up.

When I walked around the corner into the kitchen,

Greg stopped what he was doing and just stared. *Maybe I've overdone it?* He whistled.

"Wow. You look beautiful!" He came closer, wrapped his arms around my waist, and gave me a kiss. "You smell great too." Another kiss and we were off to pick up Mom.

Although solemn and sad, the funeral was very nicely done. It was nice to meet other members of George's family, but mostly it was a reunion of sorts for the neighborhood. Doreen, Margie, Arthur and Mildred, and a slew of other neighbors all came to pay their respects. Several people came up and thanked me for finding the bad guys. Of course, I don't really think I 'found' them, but I was happy to help my mom's friends and was happier to know that the drug ring had been broken up in their community.

We learned from one of the out-of-town family members that George died of natural causes and there was no foul play suspected. That helped squelch that rumor, and I was very happy to hear Leon wasn't responsible. Don't get me wrong, I want him to get his prison time for the squatting and for drugging George, and most definitely for the drug dealing he was accused of. I'm just happy to learn that George wasn't actually killed.

After spending the whole morning and part of the afternoon with Mom and her friends, we picked up Shadow and made our way over to the Johnson's. Sasha and Bella were already there, everyone in swimsuits and enjoying a warm summer's day in the pool. We had brought a change of clothes with us and were eager to join in on the fun.

After Alexis blended up a pitcher of peach daiquiris, we followed her out the sliding glass doors.

"I hope it wasn't too much to invite an extra person?"

I asked her.

"Greg? Nooo...."

"No, remember I asked Sage to come join us, too?" I laughed. "I thought it would be good for her to meet Sasha—seeing that she's going to be a character witness and helping to establish that Sasha's incident wasn't a first for Russell, er, *Milo*."

"Ohhh, that. Of course, it's okay. I know Sage from the spa...I've always liked her. I agree, I think she and Sasha will have a lot to talk about."

I checked my watch. "I hope she'll come. It's a little bit of a drive for her, but I'm sure she will."

We poured drinks into plastic glasses, and Greg and I jumped in the pool. The water was so refreshing when it was 110 degrees outside. Early August and we still had a couple more months of this. It's always the time of year that I wind up asking myself why I live here. However, no matter how hot it gets during summer, once winter hits, we all tend to develop amnesia and forget all about summer.

JJ swam over to where Greg and I were, leaving the kids playing volleyball in the shallow end of the pool.

"Guess who made detective?" he smiled widely.

"Hey! Congratulations!!" We both held up our glasses and toasted, even though JJ didn't have a drink with him. Alexis noticed and brought him one at the side of the pool before going back inside to answer the doorbell. We toasted again.

"So, Milo was Russell all along?" I asked.

"Big K—Russell Kartwood, yep! I had my suspicions early on when some tips came in, and that was also where we knew a drug cartel was operating. The hard part was finding the person himself. He didn't come out much and he used runners for all the drug activity. That's how Violet and Leon got caught up with him. He must have really trusted them, because no one else in his ring ever admitted to having seen his face. They were terrified of him and didn't want to meet him."

"I'm still amazed that Leon played like he was Mr. Knight's son. That was bold. We just got back from his funeral; heard that he hadn't been murdered, thank goodness." I took another sip of my drink before noticing that Alexis was leading Sage out into the backyard. I waved. She introduced her to everyone outside of the pool and I saw Sage immediately engage in conversation with Sasha. That's when my attention was brought back to JJ.

"Oh Leon, yeah, he's still going to serve a lot of time. Or, at least we'll see what a jury decides, but he should. He's one bad apple."

Greg knew what I've told him of the story. "Sounds like Milo was far worse…so congratulations again on solving that cold case and getting him off the streets."

"Yeah. It's funny. He's committed a lot of serious crimes, but yet, those two—Chester and him—they are a bunch of bumbling idiots when they're together. I can almost picture them as kids in juvie and can understand how they got to be friends. They're two peas in a pod!"

"So, Milo murdered his family fifteen years ago. He's kingpin of a drug ring." I lowered my voice to continue, "And he's assaulted a couple of our friends." I nodded my head toward where Sage and Sasha were conversing on the far end of the pool deck.

"I think we've just scratched the surface, Libby. We are learning a whole lot more about this dude. I just can't believe he went so long without being captured. It's not like he was truly *hiding*. In fact, he was hiding in plain sight *and* committing more crimes while doing so!"

Greg asked, "And how did his friend fit in to all this?"

JJ took a sip of the sweet frozen drink, lifted his eyes, and said, "Oh, he's a piece too! So, he divulged that after a year or more, after the murders of Milo's family and not hearing anything from him, he thought perhaps Milo killed himself too. That was a frequent thing the new reporters said…that people in his community thought he offed himself in a cave somewhere remote. Everyone wondered 'what happened to Milo Robinson' because he essentially *vanished*. However, Chester said that one day Milo contacted him out of the blue. He was shocked. But, dating back to when they were incarcerated children, Milo saved his life. He vowed to always be there for him, so even though Chester was now a born-again Christian and mostly walking the straight and narrow, thanks to Michelle really, he knew he had to help Milo."

"Amazing. That much devotion after all that time."

"Yep, amazing is right. He helped Milo change his identity and live here undetected for a long time. Great Christian man, huh?"

Greg turned to me, "But, wait … it wasn't Milo that attacked Alexis, right?"

"It was Chester."

"Why?"

JJ rolled his eyes. "Again, this guy is a piece of work, I tell you. He told us that his sole purpose was just to scare these ladies off." He pointed to both me and Alexis who was still talking to Sasha, Sage, and Bella. "The spray painting, coming into the spa after Lexi, all of it was to scare them off. He wanted the business shut down. Wait, you know he's a registered sex offender, right?"

Greg shook his head and looked at me. "No."

"Yes. An incident that happened years ago in Ohio. He maintains his innocence in the recent serial rape case here locally. And that may be true—none of the victims have been able to identify him, but we're still working on that through DNA samples and other methods since he was masked and they couldn't see his face. Anyway, he says he felt because our ladies' business in his neighborhood was a temptation, he was afraid of what *he might do*. Uh, huh. We'll get 'em, don't worry."

"That's crazy. Their business has nothing to do with sex. Why not target a strip club or something along that line instead?" Greg was dumbfounded.

"I know. Doesn't make sense at all," I added. "I suppose this is why JJ mentions that both these guys are idiots!" I laughed.

"Well, they both will be spending life in prison now. We're done with them." JJ said.

I had a thought since I hadn't spoken to Michelle since the night of the arrests. "And, Chester's wife? You guys heard everything she was telling me in the room that night, right?"

"Sure did. And, no, we don't think she had anything to do with his crimes. Since she cooperated in the end, we can overlook the fact that she lied about the alibi. Honestly, I don't even know that she *lied*, but she did do everything that Chester told her to do. She's a victim in this as well."

"I sure hope she can get her life back on track and put all this behind her. How horrible!" Greg said shaking his head.

Just then, an errant volleyball splashed down right next

to me. I picked it up and spiked it back to Joshua and his friends. The second time it came over I realized they were asking for it—time for a good dunking. I took off for that side of the pool and grabbed my godson, picked him up high in the air, turned him around, and then dunked him. He came up laughing and squealing. Suddenly, I had two of his friends all over me as we splashed and played. Shadow was going crazy at the side of the pool, running back and forth, barking at us. Finally, she couldn't take it anymore and decided to dive right in.

Later in the evening, after the kids had gone home, Bella, Sasha, and Sage had left, and Joshua was long asleep, we still hung out lounging in the chairs around the pool. It was nice to relax and not worry for the first time in weeks. I looked around to my friends and could see the sentiment was the same all around.

"Guys, we really need to think about doing a trip together. Don't you think we deserve a vacation?" I asked.

Greg was all in. "We could take my RV and hit the road!" He looked around trying to get a buy-in from JJ and Alexis.

JJ indicated he had vacation time. Alexis' eyes widened, "Libs, you know how we've talked about bringing in some interns? We could also bring in some more veteran therapists for just a couple weeks. They offer that through the school, remember?"

I was wondering how we could all be gone at the same time. "You are right. I believe Diane and Kathleen were recently looking for more work, right? Let's see if they want to fill in—we could contract with them for a specific rate."

"Yessss. How great would it be to get out of the city for awhile!"

JJ asked, "Where would we go? Is this an all adult's trip?"

"Bring Joshua—no problem! Have you guys spent much time in Utah?" I asked. "I just love it there…"

Everyone's eyes lit up and that sparked all new conversation about Bryce Canyon, Zion National Park, Moab, and many other locations that the others had never been to. I was more than willing to plan a way for us to explore these scenic locations, and I knew for a fact Shadow would be delighted. For now, she snuggled close to my feet after a long day of playing and swimming.

Thank you for taking the time to read *Spa Shadows*. If you enjoyed it please tell your friends, and I would be so grateful if you would consider posting a review. Word of mouth is an author's best friend, and very much appreciated.

Thank you,

Jennifer Morgan

* * *

Get another free book from Jennifer—scan the code to visit her website and find out how!

Watch for the next books in this series, coming very soon!

Shadowed Treasures (summer, 2022)

Shadow Retreats (fall, 2022)

Let's connect!

Website: www.jenniferjmorgan.com

Email: jennifer@jenniferjmorgan.com

Facebook: facebook.com/profile. php?id=100076154359528

Twitter: twitter.com/JenniferJMorga3

BookBub: bookbub.com/profile/433830544

Goodreads: goodreads.com/user/show/148099219-jennifer-morgan

What's next for Libby and Shadow?

Libby has had enough. With all the recent turmoil in their lives, she and her friends agree that it's time for vacation! Libby, Shadow, Greg, Alexis, and JJ load up in their RVs and caravan to Utah. It doesn't take long before they meet the quirkiest couple. 95-year-old Eugene Walker and his third wife, 85-year-old DeeDee. While enjoying live music one evening at Lake Powell, the group cannot help but admire the infectious energy, and the spunk of this elderly pair, as they dance the night away. They are the cutest!

After befriending the spritely dancers, however, Libby and her companions become suspicious. The stories told don't add up. Eugene is particularly sneaky and secretive. After spotting the fearless travelers for the third time in yet another campground in a different town, they begin to question--*are the older pair following them*? The group wants to know, and shortly they discover there is *much* more to this innocent-enough-looking duo. When Eugene suddenly goes missing, things get complicated. Long lost relatives. Monoliths. Valuable Civil War-era treasures. It's all connected, but Libby struggles to figure out how. One thing is for sure, this vacation takes on a whole new adventure for the group.